Saltwater Between Us

Jade Black

Ink & Aether Studios, LLC

Published by Ink & Aether Studios, LLC

www.inkboundrealms.com

ISBN-13: 9781971227030 (paperback)
ISBN-13: 9781971227047 (ebook)

Library of Congress Control Number: 2026908653

Cover design by GetCovers.

First edition, 2026

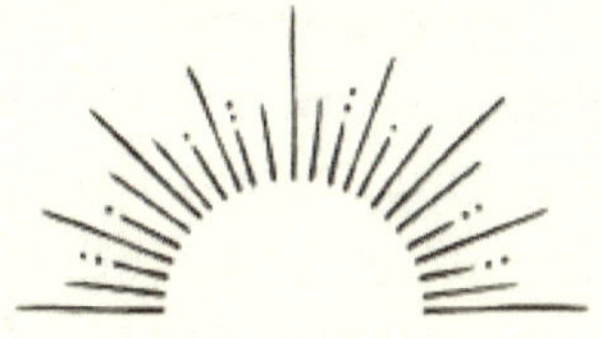

Prologue

ROXBURY, NORTH CAROLINA

Two years ago

The radio murmured low—Camila Cabello's "Havana" spilling through the speakers—and for a moment, Cerys let herself sway in her seat, hips shifting against worn upholstery, fingers drumming the steering wheel. The beat was warm. Sultry. Everything this frozen Monday morning wasn't.

Her breath misted the windshield as she killed the engine, the car's warmth bleeding away almost instantly. Outside, snowflakes drifted lazy and soft, melting the second they touched her window. The kind of snow Roxbury got maybe once a year—just enough to shut down half the city, but apparently not her office. She pulled her coat tighter and sighed.

"Havana," she muttered while getting out of her car, half-smiling. "Not exactly where I'm headed."

Her life wasn't sun-drenched cobblestone streets and ocean breezes—it was spreadsheets, fluorescent lighting, and the low hum of office HVAC.

Her phone buzzed in her coat pocket, vibrating insistently against her hip. She fished it out, already knowing who it would be before she saw the screen.

Mom.

Cerys considered letting it go to voicemail, but that would only delay the inevitable. She swiped to answer, forcing brightness into her voice.

"Hey, Mom—"

"Cerys, we really need to talk about what you're going to do."

No greeting. No preamble. Just straight to it, her mother's voice clipped and purposeful, the same tone she'd used throughout the entire estate settlement. Cerys could picture her perfectly: sitting at the kitchen table with her coffee and her planner, ready to map out Cerys' future in neat, practical checkboxes.

"I don't have time to talk right now," Cerys cut in. "I need to get to work."

"This is more important than—"

Cerys ended the call. Her thumb hit the button harder than necessary, and for a moment she just stood there in the parking lot, snow melting into her boots, staring at her mother's contact photo on the darkened screen.

Then she slid back into her car, pulled the door shut, and pressed her forehead against the steering wheel.

The scream came from somewhere deep in her chest—frustrated, raw, muffled against the cold vinyl. She let it out until her throat hurt, until the windshield fogged with her breath, until the pressure in her lungs finally eased.

When she lifted her head, she caught movement in her peripheral vision—someone two rows over, fumbling with their keys, definitely trying not to look in her direction.

Right. Professional.

She wiped her eyes quickly, straightened up, and took a breath. Then she grabbed her purse and stepped into the cold. The air bit at her cheeks, sharp enough to sting. Snow squeaked and compacted under her boots as she joined the stream of bundled-up employees trudging toward the high-rise, all of them moving with the same resigned momentum.

Pausing, she tilted her head back to look up at the building—all steel and glass and imposing angles, looming against a flat gray sky. Somewhere in her chest, something tightened.

Her grandmother's letter was still folded in her purse. She'd read it twice this morning already, tracing the shaky handwriting with her fingertips like it might unlock something.

She exhaled slowly, watching her breath hang in the frozen air, then turned and followed the crowd inside.

The elevator doors slid open with a mechanical groan, depositing her onto the third floor. The carpet—a faded maroon with geometric patterns that might have been trendy in 1992—muffled her footsteps as she navigated the narrow corridor. The finance and accounting department occupied a corner of the building that clearly hadn't seen a renovation in decades. It was crammed into a space too small for the number of bodies it held. Desks with fake wood veneer. Filing cabinets in that particular shade of "government surplus" beige. Cubicle walls upholstered in a brown tweed that belonged in a '70s catalog.

Her cubicle neighbor's voice cut through her observations.

"Morning, Cerys!" Haleigh Blake called out from her desk, already settled in with a steaming mug and her monitor glowing.

Cerys managed a smile. "Hey, Haleigh."

"So how was your weekend? I missed you last week—did you get all that stuff with your grandma's estate figured out?"

Setting her purse down, Cerys began unwinding her scarf, the wool slightly damp from the snow. "Mostly. Let's just say I've become intimately familiar with probate law and family dynamics I'd rather have avoided."

Haleigh's eyebrows drew together. "That sounds exhausting. Well, if you need any help catching up on the Morrison file or those quarterly reports, just let me know. You know how Harrison gets when things are late."

"Thanks. I appreciate it." Cerys slid her coat off and hung it on the back of her chair, then paused.

Haleigh was touching up her wrists with something from a small bottle. The scent hit Cerys a moment later—salt air and coconut, unmistakably tropical, absurdly out of place in this cramped space that smelled perpetually of stale coffee, printer toner, and the faint mustiness of old carpet.

"New perfume?"

"Oh!" Haleigh brightened, capping the bottle. "Yeah, got it this weekend. It's supposed to smell like a beach in Bali. Do you like it?"

"It's nice," Cerys said quietly. *Too nice.* The scent made something ache in her chest—a restless yearning she'd been trying to ignore for months. Maybe years.

She turned to her desk and powered up her computer, the familiar hum doing nothing to lift her spirits. The office was unusually quiet this morning—not peaceful, just *empty*. Half the staff were probably still snowed in, their desks dark, their chairs pushed in. The silence felt heavy, expectant, broken only by the rhythmic click of Haleigh's keyboard and the distant murmur of voices from Harrison's office down the hall.

Cerys glanced out the window. Gray sky, slush the color of old dishwater, gray concrete. Everything the same shade of *waiting*.

She reached for her purse and pulled out her grandmother's letter again, unfolding it carefully. The paper was soft from repeated handling, the creases worn smooth, the ink slightly smudged where her thumb had traced the words over and over.

For your adventure fund. Go see the world, Cerys. Don't wait.

Don't wait.

She could still smell Haleigh's perfume—salt and sun and freedom. Somewhere out there, people were walking on warm sand. Feeling the ocean breeze. Living.

And she was here. Staring at a mountain of paperwork in a space that still had brown tweed cubicle walls. Bracing herself for another endless week of the same.

Cerys folded the letter carefully and set it beside her keyboard where she could see it. Her fingers lingered on the edge of the paper.

The estate had been a nightmare to settle—not because her grandmother had been disorganized, but because family had crawled out of the woodwork the moment they'd heard about the inheritance: the house in Chapel Hill with its wide front porch and garden full of gardenias. The investment portfolio no one had known existed. Her grandmother's financial acumen had surprised everyone, including Cerys. It wasn't life-altering money—she wouldn't be buying superyachts or private islands—but it was *freedom* money. Enough to live modestly for a few years without working. Enough to finally say yes to all those dreams she'd been filing away in the back of her mind.

And somehow, impossibly, Gran had left it all to *her*.

Not to her mom and her siblings, who'd spent the funeral muttering about "fiscal responsibility" and "risky decisions." Not split among the cousins who'd barely visited in the last decade, who'd shown up to the wake asking pointed questions about valuations and liquidation. Just Cerys.

The letter had come with the will, tucked into an envelope with her name written in that familiar shaky script. Even now, she could picture opening it in the lawyer's office, her mother's disapproving silence heavy beside her.

Gran had always been the one with maps pinned to her walls, with stories of hiking the Appalachian Trail at sixty, of learning to sail on Lake Norman just because she wanted to know how. So Cerys had inherited the money. But not yet the bravery—sitting here in this cramped finance department, processing quarterly reports while that letter collected fingerprints.

As the day wore on, Cerys found her attention drifting—away from the Morrison file, away from the quarterly reports, away from the gray slush visible through the window. Instead, her mind wandered to places she'd only seen in photos: beaches with sand so white it hurt to look at, markets bursting with color and unfamiliar spices, streets where she'd have to piece together meaning from signs in languages she didn't speak.

She caught herself staring at her grandmother's letter again, tracing the words with her eyes. *Don't wait.*

The thing was, she'd *been* waiting. For years. Waiting for the right time, the right opportunity, the right excuse. And now her grandmother had handed her all three, wrapped in a probate settlement and a handwritten blessing.

So why was she still sitting here?

The afternoon crawled. Every email felt pointless. Every spreadsheet felt like a chain. The keys under her fingers were worn smooth in the center, the space bar slightly sticky from years of use. She could smell burnt coffee from the break room mixing with the chemical tang of printer toner, and underneath it all, that faint ghost of Haleigh's tropical perfume—a promise of somewhere else.

By four-thirty, Cerys had stopped pretending to work. She was just... sitting there. Staring at the letter.

Her heart kicked hard against her ribs.

At four forty-five, she opened a blank document. The words came easily—too easily, like they'd been waiting in her chest for months.

Dear Mr. Harrison,

I am writing to formally resign from my position, effective two weeks from today...

Her hands shook. Not from fear, exactly. From something bigger. Something that felt like standing at the edge of a cliff, toes curled over the drop.

She read it over once. Twice. Made a few edits—softened a phrase, then sharpened it again. Her cursor hovered over the "Send" button like a held breath.

One click.

Gran's voice echoed in her mind—the way she'd lived with a suitcase half-packed in the closet. The way her eyes had lit up talking about learning to rock climb just because she'd wanted to know how. That smile that had lingered even in those final days, bright and alive with memories of faraway places.

Go see the world, Cerys. Don't wait.

But what if she was making a mistake? What if this was just grief talking, not courage—what if in six months she'd be back here, begging for her old job, proving her mother right about every impulsive, irresponsible bone in her body?

The thought coiled tight in her stomach. She could feel it trying to pull her hand away from the mouse.

Then she remembered Gran's funeral. The way her mother had stood at the grave with her arms crossed, irritated by the rain. The way she'd said, "*Well, at least she had a comfortable retirement*," as if that was the highest compliment she could manage. As if a life measured in adventures and risks and sunset sails on Lake Norman could be reduced to *comfortable*.

Cerys closed her eyes and took a breath that seemed to fill her entire body. Then she clicked.

The email disappeared with a soft chime of finality.

For a long moment, she just sat there, heart hammering against her ribs, half-expecting the universe to intervene—for her computer to freeze, for Mr. Harrison to come storming out of his office, for *something* to reach through the screen and undo what she'd just done.

Nothing happened. Haleigh's keyboard kept its steady rhythm. Someone's phone buzzed three cubicles over. The HVAC system hummed on, oblivious.

And Cerys floated. Like she'd been carrying something heavy for so long she'd forgotten what it felt like to stand up straight.

She packed up her things slowly, methodically, savoring each small act of detachment. Her fingers traced the edges of worn papers, felt the smooth plastic of pens she'd been using for years. She unpinned the motivational poster she'd never actually liked—some generic sunset with *Dream Big* in swooping script. Tucked her grandmother's letter carefully into her purse. Said quiet goodbyes to the few colleagues still lingering at their desks, their faces glowing blue in the monitor light.

Outside, the cold hit her—clean, sharp, real. It stung the inside of her nostrils with each inhale.

The snow had stopped. Above her, the sky was beginning to clear, patches of pale blue breaking through the gray like promises. She could see her breath misting in front of her face, feel the crunch of snow compacting under her boots, the cold seeping through the leather and numbing her toes with each step.

Cerys tilted her face up and smiled.

She pulled her coat tighter, felt the wool scratch against her neck, and started walking toward her car. Her keys jingled in her pocket with each step. And for the first time in longer than she could remember, she felt the future stretching out ahead of her. Not as an endless gray corridor lined with cubicle walls and filing cabinets. But as an ocean—wide and blue and full of possibility.

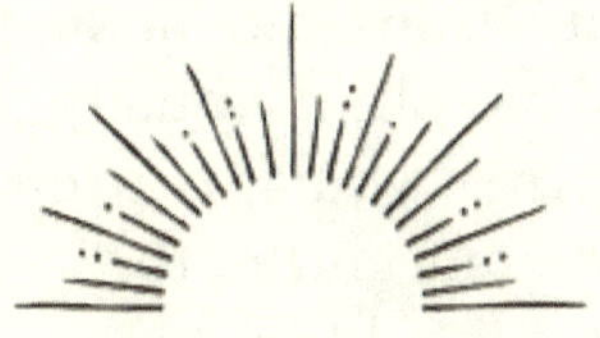

Chapter 1

Mairana Nui, Te Motu Aroha

Present Day

The morning sun warmed Cerys' dark mahogany skin as she stood at the helm of her catamaran, dark brown twists pulled into a ponytail, fiery red highlights catching the light. The breeze carried the salt-sharp scent of the sea mixed with something earthier—the smell of land after days of nothing but open water. She smiled as she reached for the linen dress draped over her chair, the fabric sun-warmed and slightly stiff from dried salt spray, pulling it on over her swimsuit.

She adjusted the sails, her body humming with the satisfaction of a solo passage. A small bird landed on the boat's railing, its bright plumage vivid against the sky, head cocking as it regarded her with one dark eye before letting out a sharp, unfamiliar trill.

Twenty-six days. She'd actually done it.

Her grandmother would've loved this.

"Land ho," she murmured to the bird, gaze lifting to the island that would be home for the next few weeks. Mairana Nui sprawled before her—rolling green hills, pristine beaches, water so blue it hurt to look at. Sailboats floated in Aroha Bay, masts swaying with the waves. Beyond the beach, traditional thatched-roof buildings nestled among modern structures with corrugated metal roofs glinting in the sunlight. Coconut palms lined the shore.

Cerys exhaled slowly. Gray towers and fluorescent lights, stale air and endless spreadsheets—all of it left behind. An ocean crossed. Alone.

And she hadn't been entirely sure she could do it.

The solitude at sea had been freeing at first—just her and the horizon. But somewhere around day fifteen, it started pressing in. Constant. Vast. Inescapable. Narrating her routine like she was still filming for her channel became the only way to hear a human voice. *Okay, so now we're going to check the rigging. Again. For the third time today because apparently I've forgotten how to trust my own work.* She'd spent too many nights talking to herself, having full conversations with the boyfriend pillow wedged into the corner of her berth.

Her last boyfriend—the one who'd wanted her to stay, to be reasonable—wouldn't recognize her now. The woman who used to need the TV on to fall asleep was gone. Now she couldn't sleep without the sound of water against the hull, the creak of lines, the subtle shift of her boat breathing with the sea.

But God, she missed conversation. Real conversation. The kind that came with eye contact and laughter and the warmth of another person sitting across from you.

As Cerys steered into the bay, the air thickened around her—humid now, clinging to her skin, carrying new scents: wood smoke, frying fish, something sweet and floral she couldn't name. A small motorboat cut through the water toward her. A young boy perched at the bow. Relief cracked through her like sunlight through clouds. Actual human beings. Her wave was perhaps too enthusiastic.

"Mālō e lelei!" The man's voice carried across the water, warm and unhurried. "Are you Cerys? Cerys Duncan?"

Paiwai Taimona. Her sponsor. Three months ago, when she'd finally committed to crossing the Pacific, she'd reached out to him through a travel forum. Having a local contact felt essential for these remote islands—not just practical, but grounding. A thread connecting her to something real.

"Mālō e lelei!" The engine cut, and the sudden silence sharpened everything—the lap of waves, the cry of seabirds, her own breathing. "Yes, you must be Paiwai."

"You made excellent time." He gestured to the boy. "This is my youngest, Turi. Throw him your lines."

The lines arced through the air. Turi secured them to the mooring ball with the unhurried confidence of someone who'd been doing this since he could walk. Father and son climbed aboard, their movements fluid and sure.

A year ago, she'd been in the Bahamas, taking day sails and telling herself she was being adventurous. Then came Ecuador. Then the decision to cross an ocean—terrifying, exhilarating. Her friends had staged an intervention. Her mother had cried. But every time doubt crept in, she'd pulled out her grandmother's letter and read it until the words steadied her again.

And now here she was, conversing with a man named Paiwai from a culture she'd only read about online. A knot of emotion tightened in her chest. Pride, yes. But something deeper too. Relief. Proof that she could trust herself this much. That leaving everything behind hadn't been reckless or foolish, but necessary.

I hope you're proud Gran.

The thought came with a bittersweet ache. How she wished her grandmother could see this—could see *her*, standing here sun-warmed and salt-crusted, having done the impossible thing. But maybe, in some way, Gran was here. In the way the wind had shifted at dawn, filling her sails without her having to adjust the sheets. In the steady pull of the lines through her calloused palms. In every micro-correction she'd made by instinct alone—tension felt before it was seen. In the courage it had taken to cast off the lines.

Cerys swallowed hard. Blinked against the brightness of the water.

She'd made it. And now came the part that scared her almost as much as the crossing itself: figuring out who she was supposed to be on the other side of it.

"My wife insists you join us for dinner," Paiwai called over his shoulder as he climbed back into his boat. "That'll give you time to get settled. We'll be back around six—I'll hail you on the radio."

"Thank you!" Cerys waved to Turi as the engine rumbled to life. "See you then!"

Back in the main cabin, she worked through her end-of-sail checklist with the kind of muscle-memory precision that came from repeating the same motions in rolling seas until they became automatic. The shower, when she finally stepped into it, felt like a small miracle. A month of quick rinses hadn't prepared her for this—the pressure, the heat, the luxury of taking her time.

Toweling off in the owner's cabin, she pulled on a fresh bikini and lounging shorts. Her hair, still damp at the ends, dripped onto her shoulders. She checked her phone—finally back in range of civilization. A handful of notifications, but nothing urgent.

She should call home. Let them know she'd made it safely.

Her mother's phone rang three times before someone picked up.

"Hello?"

Not her mother. Marcus.

"Hey," Cerys said, surprised. "What are you doing answering Mom's phone?"

"She's in the bathroom. I'm visiting." A pause. "So you made it, huh? Across the whole ocean?"

"Yeah. Just anchored a few hours ago."

"That's cool. Real adventurous!" His voice pitched up with exaggerated enthusiasm. In the background, she could hear a child's high-pitched shriek, then laughter. "So hey, listen—since I've got you. I know things have been tight for you, but I'm in a bit of a bind. Could you spot me a couple thousand? Just until—"

"Marcus, you know I don't have any money."

"Come on, Cerys. You had enough to buy a boat and sail around the world playing sailor."

"I've been over this with you. Gran left me that money specifically for this. The boat, the trip—"

"The inheritance should've been split." His voice hardened. "You know that's what would've been fair."

Cerys moved to the galley, hands finding the familiar work of rinsing out her coffee mug. The repetitive motion steadied her breathing.

Before she could respond, she heard her mother's voice in the background, then the rustle of the phone changing hands.

"Cerys? You're there?" Her mother's silky tone carried that familiar edge. "Marcus told me you made it safely. That's good. That's a relief."

"Yeah, Mom. I'm fine. The crossing went smoothly."

"You know, your brother has a point. That money could've been invested in his business. He has a family to feed, Cerys. Unlike you."

Cerys set the mug down carefully in the drying rack, watching water drip onto the counter. Took a breath. "It's his fourth business in as many years."

"That's not fair. He's trying. He's working hard to provide for his children." A pause, then her mother's voice shifted—softer now, wounded. "I just don't understand why you're doing this to yourself. To us. You're going to miss the holidays again this year. Spending time with strangers instead of your own family."

"I invited you and Dad to come out," Cerys said evenly. "I told you I'd restructure my plans, meet you in New Zealand or Australia. We could spend Christmas there together."

"That's out of the question. You know your father can't travel that far, and I'm not leaving him here alone during the holidays." Her mother sighed, heavy and pointed. "You're too old to be wasting your life like this, Cerys. Traveling around the world like you're on some gap year. You're not twenty anymore. And when something happens to you out there—because it will—we won't be around to bail you out."

The words landed with physical force—a tightness in her throat, a heaviness settling into her chest.

"I need to go, Mom." Cerys kept her voice steady. "I just wanted to let you know I arrived safely."

"Of course you do. Well. I'm glad you're safe. For now."

The line went dead.

Cerys set the phone down on the berth and stared at it for a long moment. Her chest felt tight. That old familiar ache—the one that came from wanting something from people who would never give it.

She looked around the cabin. Her cabin. On her boat. In a bay halfway across the world from everything that had tried to keep her small.

The unmade berth called to her.

After nearly a month at sea—and that phone call—she had so much to do.

Like taking a nap.

An hour and a half later, the gentle rock of the bay woke her. She stretched until her joints popped. The boyfriend pillow lay wedged against the bulkhead.

She checked her watch. Still plenty of time before Paiwai's call.

She spent the remaining time cleaning the boat, music drifting from the speakers as she scrubbed salt from the decks and restored order to the cabin. The simple routine felt grounding after weeks at sea.

The radio crackled. Paiwai's voice announced their arrival.

She rinsed off, changed, and climbed into her dinghy.

At the dock, a faded sign read 'Matariki Dock.' Another: 'Arohanui. Population: 5,000.' Paiwai and Turi waved from the main dock, silhouettes against the setting sun.

Their car bumped along a narrow road through jungle, emerging at a cluster of homes. Paiwai parked in front of a house reminiscent of the rustic homes she had seen in Panama, its metal roof glistening under the golden rays of the setting sun. The door stood open—a little girl played in the backyard with two small dogs, silhouettes dancing against a bonfire's glow.

As Cerys climbed out, a tall young man appeared down the road.

"Kae! You made it!" Turi called. "This is my older brother."

Kae's warm, tawny skin glistened with perspiration, dark eyes sparkling with welcome under the fading sunlight.

"Of course I made it. Māmā would kill me if I hadn't." He extended his hand. "You must be the guest of honor."

His hand was warm and calloused, his grip firm but not crushing. He had the relaxed confidence of someone who knew exactly where he belonged.

"That's me. Cerys Duncan."

"Hope you're hungry," Kae said, turning toward the house. "Māmā's been cooking all day. She'll expect you to clean your plate."

Inside, warmth enveloped her. Spices wafted from the kitchen, sharp and enticing, making her stomach growl in a way the bare meals on her boat never had.

A woman appeared from the kitchen in a vibrant patterned dress, directing a small army of teenagers and young adults as they laid out dish after dish on a large wooden table. "You must be Cerys!" she called warmly. "I'm Anahera. Welcome, welcome!" She gestured around the bustling room. "Some of these are ours, some belong to my sister and her husband—but they're all family."

The warmth hit her first—bodies and voices and the rich smell of spices layering the air. After weeks of silence broken only by wind and water, the sheer volume of *people* felt almost physical. Conversations overlapped. Children laughed. Someone dropped a plate in the kitchen with a clatter that made her flinch.

"Thank you so much for having me." The words came out more carefully than she'd intended, like she was remembering how to shape sentences for an audience. "This looks and smells amazing."

Kae pulled out a chair. The small gesture—so ordinary, so considerate—caught her off guard. She'd been alone so long, making every decision, managing every task. Having someone anticipate her need felt foreign. She smiled her thanks and settled into the seat, hyperaware of the way the family moved around each other with easy familiarity.

The dinner unfolded in a symphony of overlapping stories, gentle teasing, and laughter. Cerys found herself nodding along, smiling at the right moments, but slightly half a beat behind—like she was watching from just outside the frame, relearning the rhythm of communal life.

She dug into the meal, savoring flavors both foreign and wonderful. Around the table, she watched Paiwai's easy affection with Anahera. The way this family moved around each other—passing dishes without asking, finishing each other's stories, hands reaching across the table in gestures worn smooth by years of repetition.

Something in her chest pulled taut, then released—not quite an ache, but close.

The air in the room seemed to settle differently around her. A sense of belonging. But more than that—an opening. A readiness.

For what, she didn't yet know.

Chapter 2

Dawn broke soft and gold over the bay. Cerys sat cross-legged in the open-air lounge at the stern of her catamaran, equipment spread before her—cameras, memory cards, laptop. The air was still cool, but the sun was beginning to warm her shoulders. She nursed her coffee and watched the progress bar inch forward on her latest Ztube upload.

Before the boat, before the inheritance, there had been nothing worth capturing—just the same fluorescent-lit cubicle, the same commute, the same hollow routine day after day. But now she had *this*—open ocean, uncharted islands, a life worth documenting. The ocean had stripped something away, and what remained was sharper. Truer.

An hour later, she motored her dinghy toward the dock, the water glassy and calm on this side of the island.

As she approached, she spotted Paiwai waiting near the end of the pier, hands on his hips, watching her with that easy smile of his.

"*Mālō*!" she called out, her voice carrying across the water.

Paiwai caught her lines with the easy confidence of someone who'd been securing boats since childhood, his movements efficient and unhurried. "All done with your chores?" His eyes crinkled with warmth. "Nice boat you've got there. Keep her nice, you hear? She deserves it."

"Always." Cerys tossed her backpack and a small trash bag onto the dock, then stepped up beside them. The sun-warmed wood felt solid beneath her bare feet after weeks of nothing but her boat's deck. She sat to pull on her tennis shoes, glancing up at him. "Are you here on business?"

"No." His smile widened. "I saw you heading in and came out to see you."

It had been so long since anyone had simply *shown up* for her.

"Me?" The word came out lighter than she intended. Her hands paused on her laces. "Why?"

Paiwai's expression softened. Something almost paternal. "How was your first night?" He gestured toward the bay behind her, morning light catching on the calm water. "The waters weren't too bad, were they?"

She pulled on her backpack. Mountains rose beyond the harbor—still hazy in the morning light, their peaks softening against the endless blue. A bird called from somewhere in the trees lining the shore, its cry sharp and unfamiliar. Past the marina offices, the fish market already bustled with activity. Vendors arranged their morning catches on beds of ice while buyers haggled in rapid-fire Taviani. The smell of salt and diesel mixed with something sweet—*frangipani*, maybe, from the trees clustered near the customs office.

"Absolutely perfect," she said. "The mountains block the wind beautifully."

It was more than perfect, actually. She'd woken to the *tiretire*—honey-eaters—instead of alarm clocks, to the gentle rock of her boat instead of the hum of traffic. For the first time in weeks, she'd felt *settled*.

Paiwai led her toward the marina entrance. Their footsteps crunched on gravel as the path wound upward. The fish market was in full swing now. Ice scrapers rang against metal bins. The sharp smell of fresh tuna mixed with diesel and salt air. Beyond the customs office, someone grilled *ika mata* for breakfast. The scent of coconut cream and lime drifted on the breeze. Distant surf rumbled beyond the breakwater.

"Atamai says bad weather is on the way."

"Atamai?" She frowned, glancing back at the horizon. The sky was impossibly blue, the water calm. Her weather app certainly hadn't mentioned anything dramatic.

He turned back, his expression gentle but certain. "He's one of the elders. He knows these things."

She nodded. When an island-born person was said to 'know these things,' they undoubtedly *knew* those things.

Paiwai took her trash bag and tossed it into a nearby bin. "I'll give you a ride," he said, gesturing toward his car. "Anahera insisted."

They drove in comfortable silence at first, then Paiwai began sharing stories while Cerys asked questions. The landscape shifted as they climbed. Dense forest gave way to terraced hillsides. Mountains rose on either side.

Paiwai slowed the car, pausing mid-story about a hidden waterfall.

"Kae and his friends are just up that trail." He pointed to a narrow path disappearing into the trees. Cerys eyed the steep incline—muddy in places, lined with exposed roots.

"Stay on the path," Paiwai said, his voice suddenly serious. "The *ngahere*—the forest—she's protective. We don't want to lose you."

She nodded and waved him off, tightening the straps of her backpack. She adjusted her camera settings and hit record.

"*Mālō e lelei!* Just got dropped off by my host. About to hike up and meet his son and some friends. Kae promised me excellent waves, so let's see if he delivers."

She flipped the camera to capture the path ahead. The forest swallowed her quickly. Birds called from the canopy. Leaves rustled. Somewhere in the distance, surf rumbled.

She should stay on the trail. Paiwai had been clear.

But twenty minutes in, curiosity tugged her sideways. A gap in the undergrowth. A glimpse of sky beyond the next outcrop.

She paused, one foot still on the worn path, the other already angled toward the gap in the trees.

What would Gran do?

The answer came immediately, accompanied by the memory of her grandmother's mischievous smile, the one that always appeared right before she suggested something slightly scandalous or wonderfully impulsive.

Gran would absolutely leave the path.

Gran, who'd backpacked through Southeast Asia in her fifties. Who'd still been scuba diving at seventy. Who'd told Cerys, over and over, that the best stories never came from staying where you were supposed to.

Cerys smiled and stepped off the trail.

Just a little detour.

The moment she left the path, the forest closed around her. Humidity pressed against her skin. Vines snagged her ankles. The ground shifted—mossy stones slick beneath her shoes, leaf litter concealing roots that threatened to twist her feet. She pushed through, palms scraping bark as she steadied herself.

Her breath quickened. The land pushed back.

When she broke through onto the rocky overlook, the view stopped her.

The ocean stretched endlessly, sapphire-blue and glittering. Waves crashed against dark rocks below, sending up plumes of white spray that dissolved into mist. Wind tugged at her hair, her clothes, carrying salt and something sweet. Frangipani, maybe. Or something wilder.

She stood there, pulse thrumming in her throat, salt wind pulling at her edges.

She reached for her camera, lifted it—then lowered it again.

Some moments you had to live first.

Her chest felt wider than it had in months. Like something caged had finally stretched its wings.

"Right." She pulled out the compact drone, nestling her pack against a moss-covered rock. "I've got to get footage of this."

As she released it, the drone battled the gusts sweeping up from the ocean—buzzing like an angry hornet, fighting for altitude before bursting through the turbulence.

On the small screen, she noticed a group of people gathered on a beach below.

"That must be Kae and his friends." She recognized the tall silhouette. "Which means I'm not too far off course."

Through the screen, she made out the group. Two men stood near Kae, traditional tattoos dark against their skin. Another man operated his own drone nearby, his skin as deep as polished ebony. Beyond them, a cluster of figures watched the surf: women in bright bikinis, a fair-skinned man, and one surfer still in the water, his olive-toned body catching the light as he carved through a wave.

The surfer rode nearly to shore before diving off, board in tow. She leaned closer, mesmerized by how he moved—effortless, powerful, completely at home. Something in her chest caught. A breath she hadn't meant to hold.

She blinked, pulled her focus back to the screen.

She didn't notice her drone drifting lower. Didn't realize how close it had gotten until the surfer reached up and snatched it from the air.

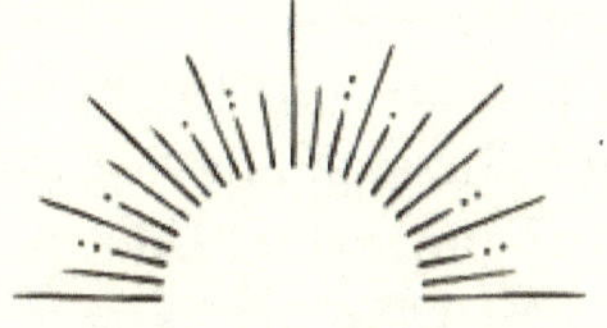

Chapter 3

"Oops," she muttered, quickly powering down the drone and stuffing everything into her pack. Small rocks skittered down the slope as she half-ran, half-slid toward the group below.

"Sorry!" she called out, slightly breathless as she picked her way over shells and driftwood. The beach was already crowded with surfboards propped in the sand like a colorful fence, and the smell of coconut sunscreen mixed with salt air. "Still kind of new at this."

"Finally made it," Kae looked up, grinning. He gestured to the group gathered near a cluster of weathered rocks. "Everyone, this is Cerys. This is my *Hoa*, Nahi Karaka—his folks have the best stall in the market. And this is Tama Rakena, he's in a band."

He gestured toward the foreign visitors. “These four arrived last week. Myles, Terry, Nadia, and Finlay from England. They’re also on Ztube.”

The last man in the group held her drone. Tall. Broad-shouldered. The small device looked absurd in his hands—delicate as a butterfly he’d plucked from the air.

“And this is Liam Taimona,” Kae added. Liam ran his free hand through damp, dark hair that curled at the ends, water still glistening on his shoulders. Traditional tattoos wrapped both arms, stark against sun-warmed skin. “You remember me telling you about him?”

“The cousin.” An apologetic smile. “Sorry about the drone ambush.”

He grunted—somewhere between amused and annoyed—and held out her device. When she reached for it, he kept his grip a moment longer, eyes locked on hers. Something flickered there, playful and sharp.

A tug freed it. “Thanks.”

Her stomach did an unexpected flip. Right. Okay.

“Thanks for sending your dad to pick me up,” she said, turning to Kae.

“No worries.” He gestured toward the others. “We’re heading to another cove if you want to come.”

“I promise to keep the drone under control this time.”

Myles stepped closer, positioning himself between her and Liam. “What model is that, by the way?”

The group gathered their things. Myles talked about camera specs—ISO ranges, frame rates, the usual. Cerys nodded along, trying to focus. But her gaze kept sliding past him to where Liam stood wringing salt water from his shorts. He then started running a towel over his broad chest, board shorts riding low enough to derail whatever question Myles had just asked.

Oh, come on. Get a grip.

But honestly—how was she supposed to concentrate when he looked like *that*?

She blinked, refocusing on Myles. Boyish. Sweet. Perfectly nice Myles. And yet her attention kept drifting back to Liam—the rough edge of his jaw, the way he moved like he belonged to this place in a way she never could.

Right. So apparently she'd been alone on that boat *way* too long.

"So you're here alone?" Nadia asked, falling into step beside her as they started up the trail. Fiery red hair whipped across freckled skin. "Seriously?"

"Uh, yeah." Cerys laughed, following Kae into the jungle. The temperature dropped immediately under the canopy, shade pressing cool against her sun-warmed skin. Birds called overhead—sharp, insistent sounds. Wet earth and green things filled her lungs. "What about you guys? Kae mentioned you came last week—group adventure?"

"Not exactly," Finlay said from ahead, stumbling slightly over a root. "My parents are funding a summer getaway. I threatened to take a gap year after high school, which apparently terrified them into agreeing to annual trips if I kept my grades up."

Terry laughed, her piercings catching fragments of light through the leaves. "So this year we landed in Tahiti, got bored after a week, and Myles heard about these islands. We chartered a boat and here we are."

"I can't imagine doing that trip alone," Nadia said, glancing through the trees toward the ocean. Salt air mixed with jungle rot, sweet and sharp at once. "It took forever on the yacht at full speed."

"I don't know." Myles met Cerys' eyes, curious. "Sounds pretty cool to me. Have you been sailing long?"

"She's a newbie," Kae called from the front. "But Pāpā said she sailed into the bay like a pro."

"Must have some islander blood in you," Liam said from behind her, his voice carrying over the rustle of leaves and the distant crash of surf. "Either that or you're reckless."

Cerys glanced back. His smirk caught her off guard—warm, playful, impossible to ignore. "Maybe both," she said, raising an eyebrow. "Kae mentioned you made your first crossing solo at eighteen. Pot, kettle?"

He shrugged, a hint of pride warming his features before his expression turned guarded. "Sailing's in our blood. I was raised on the water."

"In America, right?" Nadia moved back to walk beside him, her voice bright with interest. "That's so cool that you come here every year. We went to California last year—the surf was incredible."

The path narrowed as it climbed. Birds called from the canopy—cries that seemed to announce their passage. The distant rumble of surf grew steadily louder, punctuated now by something else: voices, laughter, the occasional whoop of triumph.

Salt overtook green. Wind cut through the humidity. Cerys felt it on her skin before she saw the opening ahead.

Minutes later, Kae stopped where the trail opened onto sand. "Alright, as promised—some of the best waves on the island."

The ocean stretched before her. Raw power. Waves crashed against the shore in explosions of white spray, her heart matching the rhythm of the surf. The beach curved in a wide arc, black volcanic rocks jutting from the sand at either end like sentinels. A handful of local surfers were already in the water, their movements fluid and precise—reading the waves with the kind of intimacy that came from a lifetime spent here.

"Wow," she breathed, turning to Kae.

"Right?" He grinned and pointed toward the surfers. "This is *Te Ngaru Kaha*—the Strong Wave. Feel like giving it a try?"

A laugh escaped as she unclipped her camera. The weight of it familiar in her hands, grounding. "I think I'll stick to filming for now."

The others headed toward the ocean, surfboards tucked under their arms. Sand warm beneath her feet, dotted with shells and fragments of coral. Her viewfinder found Liam almost automatically—tracking him as he waded into the shallows, the water rising to his waist, then his chest.

Oh, for chrissake. Powerful, easy strokes carried him out. *This is ridiculous.*

She couldn't look away. He moved like he'd been born in the water—powerful and fluid at once, reading the ocean like it was speaking a language only he knew. Kae and Myles were good, athletic and confident. Nahi and Tama had that quick, precise style that came from years of practice.

But Liam was something else entirely.

A wave rose. He caught it, stood in one smooth motion—body coiling, releasing. The board carved through water, spray catching light like scattered diamonds. Effortless. The kind that only came from doing something a thousand times until muscle and ocean became one.

Her camera rose. Record. *For content*, she told herself. *Just capturing good footage.*

Sure, her brain supplied. *That's definitely why your heart's doing that thing.*

Minutes passed—rhythmic crash of waves, calls of encouragement, sunlight turning spray to gold. Then the camera lowered. Salt spray cool on sun-warmed skin. The ocean's rhythm matching something deep in her chest, loud and insistent.

This. The word rose unbidden, felt in her bones, in the way her breath matched the swells.

Movement pulled her attention back. Liam paddled in, water streaming off his shoulders as he walked up the beach.

"Alright, enough stalling." Sand clung to his calves. He tilted his head toward the waves. "Your turn."

Blink. "I'm sorry, what? I don't know how to do..." A vague wave at the others. "...any of that."

"You *are* the woman who sailed halfway around the world by herself, right?" Water dripped from his hair, leaving dark spots in the sand. At her nod, he grinned. "Then you can handle this. Come on."

Oh god, she thought as he grabbed his board. *This is happening.*

Before she could overthink it, Cerys found herself wading into the surf behind him. The ocean floor dropped away beneath her feet—first sand, then smooth rock, then nothing. Foam swirled around her thighs, tugging with each receding wave. Liam steadied the board as she climbed on, his hands warm and solid against her waist, callused palms rough through her swimsuit.

"I'll guide you from here," he said, voice close and steady beside her as she paddled. Salt water lapped against the board. "Just focus on staying balanced."

"Please tell me you moonlighted as a surf instructor in college."

"Nope." His grin was infuriatingly confident, water dripping from his hair. "But don't worry. I've got you."

Turquoise shifted to deep sapphire, and suddenly the swells rolling toward them looked massive—nothing like the gentle ripples they'd seemed from shore. Cerys' heart hammered against her ribs.

"When the wave comes, paddle hard," Liam said. His hand brushed her ankle as he treaded water, steadying the board. "Then pop up fast—don't think, just move."

A swell approached. Dark green. Building. *Gran, if you're listening, please don't let me drown out here in the middle of nowhere.* Cerys dug her arms into the water, shoulders burning, spray stinging her eyes and nose.

"Now!" Liam's shout cut through the roar. "Stand up!"

She pushed up—too slow, weight wrong—and pitched sideways. Water slammed into her. Salt flooded her mouth. She tumbled, disoriented, lungs tight, before the ocean spat her back.

When she surfaced, gasping, Liam was right there. Laughing. "Not bad for a first try."

"Liar," she choked out, grinning despite herself. Heart pounding. Adrenaline sharp in her veins. "Again."

The afternoon blurred into wipeouts and near-misses. Each tumble sharpened her focus, her body learning the rhythm. Brine stung her throat with each wipeout, sharp and bracing. Board slick under her palms. Three glorious seconds upright before crashing again, laughing as she surfaced.

And somewhere between the fourth wipeout and the tenth, she realized: she hadn't thought about Gran in hours. Hadn't replayed the funeral. Hadn't felt that familiar weight pressing against her ribs. For the first time since she'd left, the ocean wasn't just drowning out the noise—it was replacing it with something else entirely.

This.

By the time the sun started its descent, they paddled back. Cerys collapsed onto sand still warm from the day's heat. Limbs heavy, loose. Chest light.

Sunset bled across the sky—amber, rose, deep orange. The last few surfers carved through golden light, silhouettes sharp and perfect against the glow.

Liam dropped down beside her, board dripping, sand clinging to the wax. "So. Ready to trade your sailboat for a surfboard?"

Laughter escaped. She shook her head. Wet hair stuck to her neck. "I think I'll stick to sailing." Pause. Horizon watching. "Though ask me again at the end of my stay. I might be going pro."

A chuckle, low and easy. "I could see that. Just remember who taught you everything you know."

Cerys pushed to her feet, brushing sand from her thighs. Wet fabric clung. In the fading light, Liam looked almost unreal—gilded at the edges, salt-crusted and backlit like something the island had conjured just for her. *Stop it.* Gaze forced back to the horizon. *You've known him for approximately five minutes.*

"Thanks for the lessons," she said, meeting his eyes again. "I owe you one."

"Consider it a tab." His smile turned playful, one corner of his mouth lifting. "Don't worry, my rates are cheap."

"Now you tell me." She raised an eyebrow. "You take eCash?"

"Only if it comes with a home-cooked meal." His expression shifted—a moment of vulnerability breaking through before his usual confidence returned. He tilted his head slightly. "What are your plans for tomorrow?"

The moon had started its climb, pale against the deepening blue. Cerys glanced at the darkening ocean, then back at him. "I don't usually plan. I just go with the vibe."

"Why?" she added.

"Just be ready at dawn." A mischievous glint sparked in his eyes. "And wear shoes that can handle a hike."

Cerys hesitated, weight shifting on her sand-crusted feet. Going off alone in the jungle with a man she just met probably wasn't the smartest idea.

WWGD? The thought rose unbidden. *What would Gran do?*

Gran would've gone. No question. She'd have sized him up with that sharp look of hers, asked a pointed question or two, then marched straight into whatever adventure was being offered. But she also would've made sure someone knew where she was going. Bold, not reckless.

Cerys wasn't trying to be her grandmother. Wasn't trying to replicate her exact choices or channel her spirit like some kind of séance. But maybe she could borrow a page from Gran's book—the one that said life was meant to be lived, not just observed from a safe distance.

Still. The hesitation lingered, practical and sharp in her chest.

Myles appeared from the trail before she could respond, board under one arm. “Count us in!” Already grinning. “My subscribers are dying for island content!”

Liam’s jaw tightened. Something shifted behind his eyes—annoyance, maybe disappointment. *Oh, that’s interesting.* Cerys bit back a smile and glanced between them. “Alright then. See y’all at dawn.”

As she turned toward the trail, she caught Liam’s quiet sigh behind her—barely audible over the surf, but there. Like the ocean itself pulling back from shore.

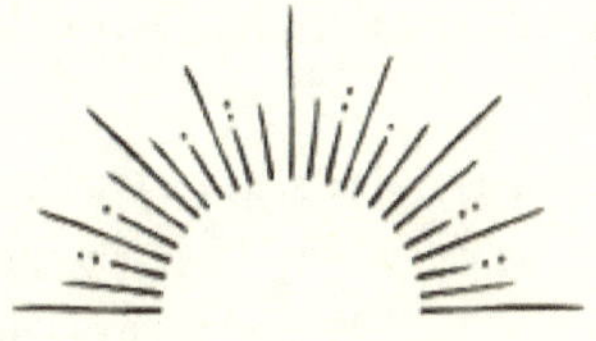

Chapter 4

The phone buzzed against worn wood—sharp in the morning quiet. Liam had been watching first light bleed across the ocean, coffee cooling in his hand, when the vibration cut through the stillness.

He glanced at the screen. *Mom.*

Of course.

"Hey, Mom."

"Liam!" Her voice, bright and sharp, sliced through the island peace. "Finally. I've been trying to reach you for days."

"Reception's spotty out here." Coffee, lukewarm now. Eyes on the horizon. "You know that."

"That's exactly my point." Static crackled with her sigh. "Why you insist on going back to that place every year is beyond me. Everything moves a hundred times slower there. You could be home, doing something productive."

The old wood creaked as he leaned back. "That's kind of the point, Mom."

"The point is to be eaten alive by bugs? Because that's all I can imagine you're doing out there in the jungle."

A smile tugged. "The bugs aren't that bad."

"Mm-hmm." Pause. Then the inevitable turn. "So when are you going to get married and give me grandchildren? I'm not getting any younger, Liam. If you spent more time at home instead of disappearing to that island, you'd actually meet a nice girl and settle down."

There it was. Same conversation, different words. The mug found the table. His temple got rubbed. "Mom—"

"I'm serious. You're thirty years old. Your father and I were already married with a baby on the way by your age."

"Different time." Voice even. Patient. "How's Dad doing?"

Another sigh—softer this time. Conceding. "He's fine. Hold on, he wants to talk to you."

The phone shuffled, muffled voices in the background. Then his father's deeper, quieter tone came through. "Liam."

"Hey, Dad."

"How's everyone doing out there?" Genuine warmth in the question. "You been surfing? How are Paiwai and Anahera?"

Liam's shoulders relaxed. "Everyone's good. Strong. Anahera's garden is incredible this year—you should see the taro. And yeah, I've been surfing. Waves have been perfect."

"Good, good." A pause. "What about Kae? He make a decision yet about college in America?"

"Not yet." A seabird skimmed the water's surface. "He's still thinking it over."

"Tell him to take his time. Big decision." His father's voice carried a weight Liam recognized—the echo of his own choice, made decades ago. "You know, I should've come with you this year."

Something squeezed in Liam's chest. "Yeah. You should have."

"I couldn't leave your mother, you know how she is." A soft exhale. "Maybe next year."

That's what you say every year. The words stayed locked behind his teeth. A glance at his watch. "I should go, Dad. Meeting a friend."

"A friend?" A thread of amusement wove through his father's tone. "Huh." A beat. "A *female* friend?"

A small smile tugged at Liam's mouth. "Yeah, Dad. A female friend."

"Well." His father chuckled, warm and knowing. "Don't let me keep you then. Say hi to everyone for me."

"Will do."

"And Liam?" A pause. "Enjoy yourself out there. You deserve it."

The call ended. Liam sat motionless, phone cooling in his palm. Through the open windows came the island's morning symphony—palms rustling their dry-leaf whisper, surf's distant percussion, the layered calls of honeycreepers and fruit doves. The world his father had left behind. The world Liam returned to every year, chasing something that lived in his chest without a name.

The cold coffee drained in one swallow. Inside, his pack hung by the door—water bottles, sunscreen, the usual. The morning stretched ahead, thick with salt air and promise and—if he let himself admit it—thoughts of Cerys that had kept him staring at the ceiling until well past midnight.

His mother's voice echoed. *If you spent more time at home, you'd meet a nice girl.*

A smile tugged as he slung the pack over one shoulder. Maybe he didn't need to go home to find what he was looking for.

Every root, every stone on the path to the dock pressed familiarly against the soles of his boots. His dinghy waited in the cove, rocking gently on its mooring. Dawn climbed higher, spilling gold across the lagoon's surface.

Salt and plumeria on the breeze. Birds calling through green shadow. And threading through it all—Cerys. How sunlight had caught in her eyes yesterday. The warmth of her skin under his steadying hands during the surf lesson, a heat that had branded itself into his palms.

Sunlight painting her in shades of amber and rose as she descended the mountain trail that first day. The image had burned itself into his memory.

The dinghy's engine turned over on the first pull. Out of the hidden cove, around the bend. A greeting called to his neighbors before heading into the open lagoon. The morning haze was already burning off, carrying the scent of hibiscus on the breeze.

Ideally, it would be just the two of them today. But he'd play nice with the college kids until Cerys was ready to focus elsewhere. Kae understood his reluctance to deal with the constant stream of tourists—this annual escape from his life in America was sacred.

He pulled up alongside her boat, admiring its sleek lines. His uncle Paiwai always said you could tell a lot about someone by their vessel. Cerys' catamaran was practical yet adventurous—much like its owner, he suspected. "Cerys!" he called out. "You ready?"

Silence. He tried again, louder. "Cerys!"

The cabin door slid open and she emerged, squinting against the sun. "Morning, Liam." Her voice carried that sleepy warmth that made his chest tighten. Loose t-shirt, shorts, hair tumbling over her shoulders. "Sorry, I overslept."

"No worries." He leaned against his boat. "Grab something to eat before we head out. Long day ahead."

"Got it." She disappeared back inside.

Liam waited, his gaze drifting across the endless blue. The ocean had always grounded him, reminded him that life extended far beyond office politics and regulatory paperwork.

When she re-emerged, she'd changed into hiking clothes, hair braided, small backpack over one shoulder. She was finishing a granola bar, eyes bright and alert.

"Ready?" She stepped into the dinghy.

He nodded and started the engine, steering toward the island.

Within five minutes, they reached the secluded beach. Liam cut the engine and vaulted over the side, pulling the dinghy onto shore. He offered Cerys his hand, steadying her as she stepped out onto the sand.

"We're heading to the highest point on the island," he said, gesturing toward the mountain rising before them. "Stay close. If you need a break, let me know. Done much hiking?"

"Not extensively," she admitted, stripping off her button-up and tying it around her waist. "Wait—I want to get this on camera. Do you mind?"

Liam leaned against a nearby palm, a smirk tugging at his lips. "Only if you make me look good."

She laughed, lifting her camera. "*Mālō e lelei ki he pongipongi ni*, everyone! I probably butchered that!" Her grin was infectious. "But it's bright and early, and I've got myself a personal guide. Right now we're standing at the base of...what's this mountain called?"

"Mount Tohivea," Liam said, pride warming his voice as he gestured toward the peak. "Also known as the Home of Mālikū—guardian god of our island. Ready to see if he's home?"

Cerys nodded, her eyes bright with determination. "Alright, let's do this." She slipped the camera into her bag and fell into step beside him as they started the ascent.

The trail began gently, winding through thick tropical canopy. Blooming flowers and damp earth perfumed the air. Liam moved ahead with the quiet confidence of someone who knew every root and stone by heart, his steps sure on the uneven ground.

As they climbed, the path steepened and narrowed. When he glanced back and saw her breathing hard, he slowed. "You're doing great," he called over his shoulder. "Almost there."

When they finally crested the summit, he heard her sharp intake of breath. The island spread below them in stunning clarity—crystal lagoon, dense jungle, and her boat bobbing like a tiny white shell far out on the water. The view never failed to move him.

"This..." Cerys breathed, stepping beside him. "This is incredible."

Liam leaned against a sun-warmed rock, watching her take it all in—the way wonder softened her features, the way the breeze caught her hair. "Thought you might like it," he said quietly. "One of my favorite spots on the island."

She moved closer, drinking in the panorama. Emerald canopy met azure sea in an endless dance of color. The breeze carried salt and sweetness, island perfume he'd know anywhere. Her eyes were wide, unguarded. He memorized this moment—her awe, this place, the two of them standing together above the world.

They stood shoulder to shoulder as the island's peace settled over him—that rare stillness where the rest of the world couldn't reach. He drew in a slow breath, letting the moment hold. "So what made you do it?" His voice came out quieter than he'd planned. "Just sail off alone across the ocean?"

Cerys turned, meeting his eyes. She caught her bottom lip between her teeth, thinking. "My grandmother died two years ago," she said finally, fingers finding a loose thread on her shirt. "She and I...well we sort of always had a shared dream." Her gaze drifted to the horizon. "Back home I felt trapped. Like I was disappearing behind a screen while life happened somewhere else." Her voice dropped. "When the chance came, I had to take it."

A seabird traced lazy circles above the jungle. "Sometimes we need to blow everything up just to remember we're alive." He looked back at her. "Takes guts to actually do it, though."

A smile touched her lips. She lowered herself to the ground, fingers trailing through the cool grass. He settled beside her—close enough that their shoulders nearly touched.

"What about you?" Cerys asked. "Kae said you've been coming back almost every year since you were eighteen. Why?"

A blade of grass appeared in his hand, turning between his fingers. "My father and Kae's are brothers," he said. "Mine left for America chasing something better. Wasn't easy—leaving or staying gone." His gaze swept the island below. "America's home. But this place..." The grass stilled. "It's like rediscovering a part of myself every year." A half-smile. "World keeps rushing forward. Nice to have somewhere that lets you just stand still."

She turned to him, eyes catching the golden light. "You ever think about staying? Full-time, I mean?"

He chuckled, still turning the grass blade between his fingers. "Every Monday through Friday." His gaze stayed on the delicate green strand. "Nah, it's not so bad. You're just seeing it through post-break up eyes."

"Post-break up eyes?"

"Yeah." He traded the grass for a small wildflower, twirling it absently. "You know, when you've just broken up with someone and everything reminds you of them. In this case, you've broken up with your life back home, so everything there seems like a bad ex-boyfriend." He brought the flower to his nose, inhaling. A soft laugh escaped him. "But trust me, the feeling will pass."

She studied him, considering. After a moment she leaned back against the rock, gaze drifting to the island spread below. "Maybe." A quiet sigh. "But I don't think so."

The moment hung between them, comfortable and weighted at once. Then her phone shattered it—a bright trill in the stillness. She straightened, fishing it from her pocket. "Sorry. It's Myles."

His own phone buzzed. Kae's text glowed on the screen: *Kāne! Tried to give you two some time but Myles is determined to get his footage. We're heading your way. Hope I didn't ruin the moment too badly.*

He rolled his eyes at his cousin's teasing, tucking the phone away.

Cerys listened a moment longer, then sighed. "They're on their way up." She offered him a rueful smile as she ended the call.

"Then we should head down and meet them." He stood, reaching for her backpack. Pebbles scattered down the slope. "Don't make plans for tomorrow. I'm taking you to a local secret." He paused, eyes glinting. "You're not afraid of sharks, are you?"

"Let me think." She closed her eyes in mock contemplation. "Yes. I am indeed incredibly frightened of them. As anyone with sense should be."

His laughter echoed off the rocks. "They're more scared of you than you are of them." He offered his hand. "Trust me, it'll be unforgettable."

At the base of the mountain, Kae and the crew approached. Myles waved, camera already in hand. "Hope we didn't interrupt anything," he said with a knowing smirk.

Cerys rolled her eyes. "Nothing that can't be continued later." Her gaze met Liam's, and he grinned.

"Where to next?" she asked.

"The cave?" Kae gestured toward the distant cliffs. "If we time it right, we can catch the slack tide."

Liam's face broke into a grin. "Perfect." He started toward the dinghy with Cerys. "You take the others," he called to Kae over the breeze. "Cerys and I will go ahead. She wants to capture some footage."

Myles appeared beside them, breathing hard from his jog. "Hold up, I'm coming with you." His camera gear bounced as he stopped. "My drone won't interfere with yours, Cerys. I need b-roll that isn't just Nadia and Terry posing on a beach."

Liam arched an eyebrow but gestured toward the boat. Soft laughter drifted from Kae and the others as they climbed aboard. He kept his expression neutral, though his jaw tightened. Patience had its limits.

The dinghy cut through turquoise water, engine thrumming beneath them. Wind caught Cerys' twists, whipping the red-threaded strands across her face as she leaned over the side, drone controller balanced in both hands. Above, two drones buzzed—hers and Myles'—capturing the coastline in overlapping sweeps.

One hand on the throttle, gaze shifting between the rocky approach and Cerys. Sunlight found every angle of her—the curve of her jaw, the concentration creasing her brow, the deliberate precision in her fingers. *Getting used to this. Shouldn't be.*

The engine's rumble died to silence as they neared the cave entrance, rocks rising dark from the water. Waves lapped against stone. The air shifted—cooler here, carrying the mineral tang of wet rock and trapped seawater.

"Here." Liam reached up as Cerys guided her drone down, steadying the device before passing it back. Their fingers brushed—brief, warm. He caught her eye and smiled before turning to include Myles. "We swim from here. Cave's water access only."

Myles shrugged, already stripping to swim trunks. Equipment clattered as he set it aside. Cerys pulled off her outer layer, revealing a sleek black suit underneath. She secured her camera in its waterproof housing.

Liam dropped the anchor. *Focus.* When the line was secure, he dove—clean arc, minimal splash. The water closed around him, cool and heavy, temperature dropping as he passed into the cave's shadow.

Behind him, Cerys and Myles followed, their strokes breaking the surface rhythm. He surfaced and struck out toward the cave mouth.

Inside, the world transformed. Stone teeth hung from darkness above, water clinging to each point before releasing in soft drops—*plink, plink, plink.* Light filtered through the entrance, fracturing across the surface in shifting patterns of blue and gold.

Cerys stood in the shallows, camera already working. The careful placement of each step. The way wonder softened her whole face. Liam let himself drift, unable to look away even as he tried to take in the cave itself.

They spread out, voices echoing off wet stone. Cerys moved deeper, camera raised, capturing the play of light on ancient rock. Myles circled with his drone remote, muttering about angles. The others wandered toward the back, where shadows pooled thick and cool.

Liam hung back near the entrance, one eye on the group, the other on the water. Something felt off. He waded closer to the mouth, studying the current's pull.

The waterline had climbed. Six inches higher than when they'd entered, maybe more. The sound had changed too—sharper echo, waves hitting stone with more force. The water tugged at his legs with purpose now, no longer the lazy drift from before.

He glanced back at the scattered group. Cerys framed another shot, completely absorbed. The ocean was deciding faster than he'd planned.

No more time to wait.

"Everyone." His voice cut through the cave's echo, sharp enough that heads turned. "Tide's moving faster than I thought." He gestured toward the back passage, tone firm, leaving no room for debate. "We're taking the land route. Kae—you know it. Take point."

Kae's expression shifted—recognition, then quick assessment. He nodded, already moving. The group fell in behind him, feet careful on slick stone. Cerys picked her way across the uneven surface, camera still in hand, focus split between her footing and the footage she'd captured.

Behind her, Finlay and Myles traded jokes, their laughter bouncing off the walls—too loud, too careless. Liam watched them shove each other, wavering on wet rock. His shoulders drew tight, muscles coiling beneath the surface. "Hey—"

But Finlay pushed too hard. Myles stumbled back, arms windmilling. Straight into Cerys.

Everything slowed. No, *not her.*

Cerys' foot slipped. Her body tilted. She twisted, trying to catch herself, but momentum won. She went over the edge.

The splash rang out like a gunshot.

Her camera slipped from her grasp, disappearing into the dark water. She surfaced, gasping, and the current seized her—dragging her toward the cave mouth with terrifying speed.

The laughter died. Finlay's face went white. "Oh god—I didn't—"

But Liam was already moving.

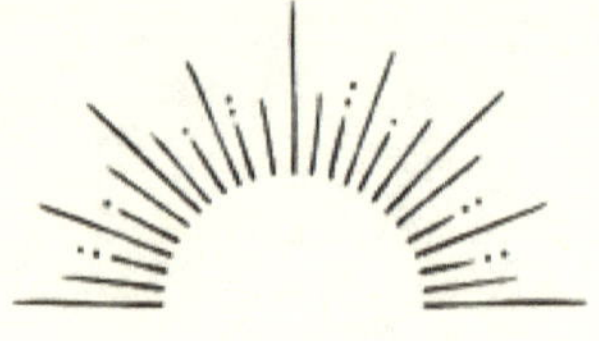

Chapter 5

"Cerys!" Liam's shout rang against stone. He dove, the impact cold and sharp.

The world above warped—muffled voices, thrashing water. Kae yelled something, but Liam had no time to parse it. Every second she was under was a second too long.

He drove deeper, eyes burning with salt. The current pulled hard, swirling sediment into murky clouds. His vision tunneled—everything narrowing to the churning water ahead, the fear clawing at his ribs.

Then he lost sight of her.

Panic flared, white-hot. He shoved it down. *Not now. Keep moving.*

He broke the surface, dragged in air. "Kae!" His voice cracked raw. "Get them out—I've got her!"

He didn't wait for an answer. One breath, then back under.

His chest locked tight. Every thought collapsed to a single point: *Find her.*

Vision blurred. Arms burning. Then—

There.

A shape in the churn. Cerys, arms flailing weak against the pull.

He closed the distance, each stroke a fight against the pull. The cold bit deeper, seeping into his bones.

The distance closed. His hand caught her arm. The relief was physical—breath returning, blood rushing. He pulled them both up, breaking the surface as she gasped and coughed, fingers digging into his shoulders.

She fought the current, panic driving her strokes wild.

"Cerys—listen." His voice cut through her fear, firm and steady. "Stop fighting it. We swim parallel. Understand?"

Her wide eyes found his. A braid floated past his face, waterlogged and heavy. She nodded, fear and trust tangled in her expression.

Something in his chest cracked open. "Trust me," he said. "I've got you." Then he started swimming.

The sea raged around them, dark water churning against volcanic rock worn smooth by centuries of tide. Liam held on, arm locked around her ribs, swimming with everything left in him. A wave hit—bigger than the rest—and swept them sideways into a narrow channel he hadn't seen, its walls streaked with rust-colored mineral deposits.

"Shit—hold on!" The words ripped from his throat. "Don't fight it!"

The channel funneled them fast, water churning white against dark basalt. His shoulder scraped rock, pain blooming hot. Cerys coughed—sharp, wet—and his grip tightened, fingers digging into her side.

Then he saw it. A break in the stone ahead. Small cave, the entrance barely above the waterline. The current pushed them straight toward it.

He kicked hard. Once. Twice. They broke through into sudden calm.

They surfaced together, gasping. The roar of the ocean dulled to a distant echo. His heart hammered against his ribs—*alive, we're alive*—and before he could think, before the adrenaline could fade, he pulled her close and kissed her. Quick. Desperate. Grounding them both in the moment they'd survived.

The cave ceiling hung low, the air thick with damp stone and salt. Through the dim light, he spotted a patch of sand beyond the jagged rocks, sheltered against the far wall.

His lungs burned. His arms shook. Salt water clung to his skin. *We made it.*

"There." The word came out rough. He nodded toward the sand, had to swallow before he could speak again. "Can you make it?"

She followed his gaze and nodded, still gasping, her whole body trembling.

He pulled himself onto the rocks first, muscles screaming. Then he turned and reached for her, hand steady despite the tremor working through his shoulders. Cerys gripped his hand, and he hauled her up beside him. They picked their way across the uneven stone until they reached the sand.

They collapsed—finally able to breathe.

For a moment, neither spoke. Just breath. The drip of water echoing off stone. His heart pounding.

The adrenaline crash hit him all at once—his whole body shaking, cold flooding through him despite the thick island air.

Liam turned his head, found her eyes already on him. Wide. Dark. Still edged with fear.

His hand moved without thought, brushing a waterlogged braid from her face. Water dripped from the strands, cold against his fingers. "You okay?"

She nodded, breath still coming fast. A shiver ran through her—whether from cold or leftover fear, he couldn't tell. "I..." A pause. Her chest rose and fell. "I don't know." Her voice shook, then steadied. "Kiss me again to check."

His eyes widened. Then he saw it—the same adrenaline thrumming through him reflected in her gaze. The desperate need to confirm they were alive. *Holy hell, we're alive.*

A soft laugh escaped him, rough and breathless. "My pleasure."

He didn't move right away. His thumb traced her jawline, slow, deliberate. Taking her in—the way her lashes clung together with seawater, the pulse hammering at her throat, the tremor still working through her shoulders. Water dripped from the cave ceiling around them. Salt stung his lips. His heart refused to slow.

Almost lost her. The thought sat heavy in his chest—her laugh from the boat ride, the way wonder had softened her whole face in the cave. His hand slid from her jaw to cup the back of her neck, fingers threading through her wet braids, anchoring himself to the warmth of her skin, to the proof that she was here, alive, breathing.

He leaned in, lips hovering over hers. The distance closed—slowly this time. Once. Twice. Soft presses that deepened into something warmer, more deliberate. The taste of salt. The warmth of her breath mixing with his.

They were sitting in the sand, close enough that their knees touched. Her hands found his chest, fingers curling into the wet fabric of his shirt. He shifted closer, his free hand bracing against the sand beside her hip as the kiss deepened—heat building between them, the way she tilted her face up to his, the soft sound she made against his mouth.

His hand slid from her neck to her waist, palm spreading across her ribcage, feeling the rapid rise and fall of her breathing. Her body arched toward him, and he could feel her heart hammering beneath his touch—matching his own frantic rhythm. His peripheral vision dimmed—everything narrowing to the feeling of her mouth on his, the way her fingers had moved from his chest to tangle in his hair.

He pulled back slightly, forehead resting against hers, both of them still half-reclined in the sand. Their breathing tangled together in the small space between them. His thumb traced along her bottom rib, unable to stop touching her, needing the contact.

"Liam! Cerys!" Kae's voice cut through the cave like a blade. "Are you in here?"

They jerked apart. Liam's hand slipped from her waist as they both scrambled to sitting positions. Cerys stumbled slightly in the sand, and he caught her elbow—steadying, automatic—then dropped his hand like he'd been burned.

"Shit," he muttered under his breath, dragging a hand down his face. His pulse still hammered, adrenaline and desire tangled so tight he couldn't separate them. The air felt suddenly cooler against his damp skin, salt-crusted clothes clinging like ice now that the heat between them had broken.

Cerys blinked up at him from where she sat in the sand, her warm brown eyes hazy, unfocused. Then awareness crept back in—a sharp inhale, shoulders stiffening. She pushed herself fully upright, smoothing her wet suit with unsteady hands.

Footsteps echoed closer—multiple sets now, splashing through shallow water. Liam exhaled slowly, willing his heart to settle. It didn't listen. Outside the cave, the ocean's roar still pulsed, a distant reminder that the world hadn't finished with them yet.

"Here!" he called out, voice rougher than intended, the word catching slightly in his throat. He pushed to his feet, muscles protesting the sudden movement, then reached down to help Cerys up. Their fingers tangled briefly—warm despite everything—before he let go.

Kae appeared at the cave entrance first, his flashlight sweeping across the space, the beam cutting through the dim mineral-tinged air. His eyes landed on them, and Liam caught the flash of relief—followed immediately by a knowing look that made him want to glare.

He did glare. Just a little.

Chapter 6

Cerys worked in the galley, hands moving through the familiar rhythm of preparing drinks. The boat swayed gently beneath her feet. Citrus filled the small space as she sliced a lemon.

Above, she could hear Liam's footsteps on deck, the soft rustle of sails. He hadn't told her where they were going—just flashed that grin and said it was a surprise.

Since the cave, days had melted into one another like watercolors bleeding across canvas. Each morning, Liam appeared at her boat with that particular spark in his eyes—the one that promised something worth leaving the galley for. They'd dived coral gardens where fish moved like living gemstones. Wandered village markets where Tahitian vanilla hung thick in the air, where vendors called out in Taviani and laughter spilled from open doorways. Evenings at Paiwai's, where the food carried the weight of tradition and the company asked nothing of her but presence.

Myles and Finlay had apologized. Multiple times. She'd waved them off, told them it was fine. And it was—mostly. The fear had dissolved like salt in seawater. What remained was harder to name.

Now, as Mairana Nui shrank behind them and open water stretched ahead, Cerys glanced over her shoulder. Liam stood at the helm, sunlight turning his skin to bronze, white shirt plastered to his shoulders by wind and spray. He guided the boat with that quiet confidence she'd come to recognize—the kind that didn't announce itself, just *was*. The sight stirred something low in her chest, a warmth that had nothing to do with the tropical sun.

The voice in her head whispered its familiar warning: *Don't get attached.* But she could feel herself tipping toward him anyway—his easy laugh that started deep in his chest, his steady presence that made even silence comfortable, the way he looked at her like she mattered. Like she was worth showing up for.

The thought of saying goodbye hurt more each day. No second coffee cup in the morning. No voice calling from the helm. Just silence and empty water.

She shook it off and focused on the drinks. Lemon, sharp and bright under her knife. Sparkling water fizzing over ice cubes that clinked against glass. Honey drizzled in slow ribbons—sweet against tart, the golden stream catching light as it spiraled down, pooling at the bottom before she stirred it through with deliberate, practiced motions.

"Drinks are ready!" She carried them carefully up to the cockpit, barefoot on the warm teak.

Liam looked up. “Perfect timing.” His gaze flicked to the glasses, condensation already forming on the sides, then back to her face. “I was just about to call you.”

She handed him one, their fingers brushing briefly. “Oh? Why’s that?”

“Gonna need to change the sails,” he said, setting the glass in the cockpit holder. “You man the helm and I’ll go up front.”

The wheel felt smooth and sun-warmed under her palms as she took his place. The boat responded—alive, eager—while he moved forward with that fluid assurance that came from a lifetime on the water. The sails snapped taut with a sound like thunder.

Speed surged through the hull. Wind whipped her hair back, salt spray kissing her skin. A laugh burst from her—pure, unguarded exhilaration.

“Alright!” His voice carried back. “Kick on the autopilot.”

With the autopilot engaged, she watched him return. He picked up his drink, raising it to her with a satisfied smile. “Not much longer.”

He stretched out on the banquette, legs extended, his dark hair swept back by the breeze. His gaze tracked the sails with easy confidence.

Her eyes lingered on the strong line of his shoulders, the way sunlight carved shadows along his arms. Since the cave, she’d caught herself wanting to touch him—to feel the solid warmth of him, to know if he’d thought about it too.

Maybe he was telling himself the same thing she was: *Don’t get attached.*

He'd go back to America when summer ended. She'd sail on to places she couldn't yet name. Different worlds. Different lives.

But god, she wanted a taste of this one.

Cerys leaned forward, fingers drumming against the bench as she pressed him again. "Come on, where are we headed? Just a tiny clue?"

His eyes crinkled. "Now, now," he drawled, voice warm like honey, "where's the fun in spoiling the surprise?" He winked.

Her chest tightened—annoying and wonderful at once.

The dashboard drew her attention, fingers tracing the navigation screen's cool surface. "Listen," she began, softer now. "About the cave..." A swallow. "I don't hold it against you. Or the others. It was an accident." Her eyes flicked to his. "You don't have to keep playing tour guide. This is your vacation too."

Liam went still. The easy grin faded, replaced by something that sent her pulse racing. He held her gaze—steady, unblinking.

"Cerys." Her name came out quiet. Almost careful. He leaned forward, elbows on his knees, closing the distance between them. "I'm here because I want to be." A pause, his eyes holding hers. Then softer, with more weight: "With you."

She opened her mouth. Closed it. Heat crept up her neck.

"The cave... that was on me. I knew better." A rueful smile tugged at his mouth. His hand lifted, then dropped back to his knee—a rare moment of hesitation. "Wanted to impress you. Lesson learned." His focus never shifted from her face. "But I'd like a chance to make it up to you."

Something warm bloomed in her chest—surprise tangled with hope she hadn't expected to feel. She smiled, the last of the day's uncertainty dissolving like salt in seawater. "Alright, Captain. Let's see where this takes us."

The horizon answered. A smudge of green appeared, growing with each passing moment.

Cerys' breath caught.

The island rose from the sea—white sand ribboning the shore, vibrant greenery climbing inland. Then she saw the rock formations that made her lean forward against the railing: massive coral-white pillars jutting from the shallows like ancient sentinels. They were worn smooth by centuries of tide, standing in water so clear she could see schools of fish moving thirty feet down, their shadows flickering across the sandy bottom.

She stood, moving to the railing. The breeze carried something sweet—frangipani, maybe, mixed with salt. " Liam... where are we?"

He came up beside her, close enough that his arm brushed hers. "Rangi Ora. Means 'Peaceful Heaven.' " He glanced at her, mouth quirking. "Those formations? They're called the Pillars of Tangaroa. Named after the sea god. Not bad, huh?"

"Not bad at all."

They changed into swimsuits. Liam lowered the dinghy, each movement economical and sure—the kind born of repetition, not thought. He offered his hand. His palm was warm, calloused. The contact sent a small spark through her.

The engine sputtered to life. They skimmed across the water, spray kissing their skin, the sun warm on her shoulders. The reef came alive beneath them—coral in impossible colors, fish darting through like living jewels.

A sea turtle glided past, ancient and unhurried. Hours blurred together: laughing, diving, Cerys pointing at formations while Liam named species she'd never seen, his voice carrying across the water between dives, the world reduced to salt and sunlight and the press of his hand steadying her when the current pulled too strong.

The sun dropped lower. They made for the beach.

Liam gathered driftwood—sun-bleached pieces smoothed by endless tides—and soon had a fire crackling. Orange and pink streaked the sky, reflecting off the Pillars of Tangaroa in the distance. The formations glowed amber in the fading light, ancient guardians watching over the lagoon.

Cerys hugged her knees to her chest, fire warmth spreading across her skin while the evening breeze cooled her back. The contrast made her hyperaware of every sensation—heat and chill, stillness and movement. She glanced at Liam. His eyes were closed, expression serene. Firelight carved shadows along his jaw. Smoke drifted between them, carrying the scent of salt and charred wood.

"Liam," she whispered. He turned, eyes meeting hers, reflecting the flames. "Thank you. For this. For everything."

His smile was soft, genuine. He reached out, fingers intertwining with hers. The touch was electric—calloused, steady. "It's getting late," he murmured, thumb tracing circles on her hand. He paused, gaze dropping to where their hands joined, then back to her face. "I should get you home."

They sailed back to Aroha Bay in silence. The kind of silence that felt full rather than empty—weighted with things neither of them was ready to name.

The moon had risen, casting a silvery path across the water. Cerys stood at the bow, watching the way moonlight fractured on the waves, each crest catching light before dissolving back into darkness. Behind her, she could hear Liam moving about the cockpit—the soft scrape of a winch, the rustle of a line being coiled. Small, familiar sounds that somehow felt different now.

She glanced back. He was focused on the helm, face half-shadowed, but she caught the moment his eyes lifted to meet hers. Neither of them looked away immediately. The air between them hummed with something unspoken.

Rigging creaked softly with the boat's motion. Waves slapped against the hull in a steady rhythm that matched her heartbeat. The night folded around them—wind cool against sun-warmed skin, the low murmur of water against the hull, Aroha Bay's scattered lights brightening as the distance closed.

When they reached the anchorage, they worked in sync to bring down the sails and set the anchor. Movements coordinated and wordless. His hand steadied her elbow as she leaned over to secure a line. Her fingers brushed his when they both reached for the same cleat. Each touch lingered—dizzying, inevitable, like the pull of the tide.

The boat settled into its gentle rocking.

Liam disappeared into the boat's interior without a word. Cerys stood in the cockpit, pulse thrumming, watching the cabin lights glow warm against the darkness. She could hear him moving below—the soft thud of a drawer closing, footsteps on the companionway.

When he emerged, he had his bag slung over his shoulder. The sight of it—him preparing to leave—sent a pang through her chest that she hadn't expected.

"All right, young lady," he said, tone playful despite the tension between them. Light from the cabin cast shadows across his face. "Remember not to stay up too late. Tomorrow is another early start. I'll take your dinghy back with me and fuel it up first thing."

Cerys stood in the doorway, fingers nervously playing with the edge of her cover-up. "Or..." she began, her voice carrying over the gentle murmur of waves.

Liam turned to face her, his dark eyes meeting hers. "Or..." he echoed, his voice low.

The space between them hummed with unspoken possibility.

Cerys inhaled. Her heart hammered. "Or you could just stay," she said. "Here. With me."

"Unless you don't want to," she added quickly.

He went still. Just for a moment—a hesitation that carried weight. His jaw tensed slightly, and she caught the flicker of something in his eyes. Conflict, maybe. Or fear of what staying meant. He drew in a slow breath, held it. Then his shoulders dropped, decision made.

He moved—swift, fluid—closing the distance between them. His hands came up to cup her face, warm and rough against her skin. His eyes held hers for one suspended moment before his mouth found hers.

The kiss was gentle. Then it wasn't.

When they pulled apart, both breathless, he rested his forehead against hers. The warmth of him surrounded her—his breath, his skin, the solid presence of him. Then he stepped back just enough to watch her face, searching for something.

"Wow," Cerys managed. Her pulse still thundered in her ears. Heat bloomed in her chest, spreading through her limbs. She wanted to say more—wanted to pull him back—but the words tangled somewhere between her heart and her throat. "So that's a yes?"

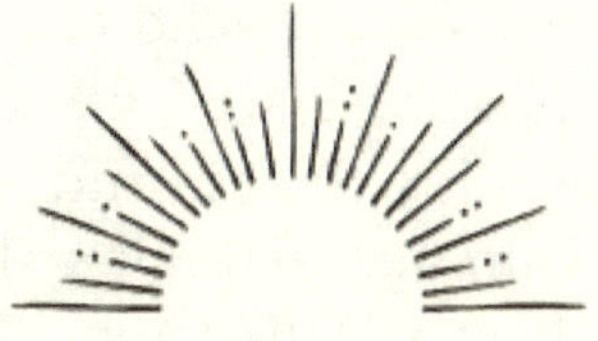

Chapter 7

His eyes held hers—dark, intent, hungry. A shiver rippled through her that had nothing to do with the night air.

“You’re cold,” he murmured, voice low and rough like gravel under bare feet. “Let me warm you up.”

Something wicked curled in her belly at the promise. “Something tells me you’re very good at that.”

A low chuckle vibrated from his chest. “Baby, I’m excellent at it.” He closed the last inch between them. “Allow me.”

His arms came around her, solid and sun-warm. Big hands skimmed down her sides, gathering the thin cover-up. One slow tug and the knot surrendered. The fabric whispered down her legs and disappeared into the breeze like a secret.

“Better?” His palms settled on her bare waist, thumbs stroking just above the line of her bikini bottoms.

"Almost." Her voice trembled with anticipation. "My turn."

She dragged his shirt up and off, letting her palms revel in the warm, salt-dusted expanse of his chest. Sun-darkened muscles flexed under her touch. She leaned in, kissed him deep—tongue sliding against his, tasting ocean and heat and the faint edge of the beer he'd had earlier.

He groaned into her mouth, the sound raw. His fingers found the knot of her bikini top and worked it loose with deliberate patience. The triangles fell away. Cool air kissed her breasts; his hot palms replaced it instantly, cupping, weighing, thumbs brushing her nipples until they tightened into aching peaks.

He pulled back just far enough to search her face, eyes almost black in the amber cabin light. "Tell me you want this, Cerys. Say the words."

"I want this," she breathed, pulling him back down. "I want your hands, your mouth... I want all of it."

The kiss turned filthy—wet, open, hungry. He lifted her without breaking it. Her legs wrapped around his waist like they belonged there. Her back met the cool salon wall for one dizzy second before he carried her to the banquette. Cushions gave beneath them. The boat rocked gently, matching the slow grind of her hips against the hard ridge straining his shorts.

"Fuck, you feel good," he rasped against her lips. "Already so hot for me and I haven't even touched you properly yet."

She rocked again, chasing friction. A broken sound escaped her. He chuckled darkly.

"Greedy girl." His mouth left hers to trail hot, open kisses down her throat. "You've been staring at me all day.

Thinking about this?" He sucked lightly at the pulse point beneath her ear. "Thinking about my tongue between your legs while you pretended to watch the sunset?"

Heat flooded her face. "Maybe."

His laugh vibrated against her skin. "Good. Because I've been hard since the moment you stepped out of the water in that tiny bikini." His tongue traced the swell of one breast, then the other, teasing the sensitive undersides until she arched, silently begging.

Only then did he close his mouth over her nipple—slow, deliberate suction that sent lightning straight between her thighs.

She buried her fingers in his damp hair, salt rough against her palms. "Damn, you're really good at this," she rasped, voice barely recognizable. "Liam... more."

He switched to the other breast, giving it the same torturous attention while his hand slid down her stomach, fingers slipping just beneath the waistband of her bottoms. He traced the edge back and forth, back and forth, never going lower.

"So impatient," he murmured against her skin. "But I'm not rushing tonight. I want to taste every inch of you first." His teeth grazed her nipple lightly. "I want to hear you moan my name until you forget every other word."

Her laughter rang out. "Oh I see, you were the kid who liked to play with your food?"

"Something like that."

The breeze picked up outside, cooler air slipping through the hatch, but inside the salon the temperature felt volcanic. He stood, lifting her again, and carried her down the companionway to her cabin. The moment her back hit the bed he crawled over her like a predator who had all the time in the world.

His mouth painted a lazy path down her body—kisses between her breasts, tongue dipping into her navel, teeth nipping the soft skin just above her bikini line. He hooked his fingers in the knots at her hips.

"Lift for me, beautiful."

She did. The scraps of fabric slid away. Cool air kissed her overheated skin, then his breath replaced it—hot, deliberate, inches from where she needed him most.

"Look at you," he said, voice thick. "So wet already. All this for me?" Two fingers parted her gently, tracing her slick folds without entering. "You're dripping, Cerys. I can see how badly you want my mouth."

She whimpered, hips twitching. "Liam...

"Āe, *ataahua*?" His voice carried that smile again. "I'm in the middle of enjoying my feast."

"Please."

"Please what?" He pressed the lightest kiss to her inner thigh. "Use your words."

"I want your tongue on me. Now."

He rewarded her with a slow, flat lick that tore a cry from her throat. Then he settled in—devouring her with devastating patience. Long, luxurious strokes. Tight circles. Gentle suction. Every time her breath hitched and her thighs started to shake, he eased back, blowing cool air across her sensitive flesh until she was nearly sobbing.

"Such a sweet little feast," he murmured, voice vibrating against her. "But I'm not letting you come yet. Not until I've had my fill." He slid one thick finger inside her, curling it slowly while his tongue kept working. "Feel that? That's just a preview of how I'm going to fill you up later."

She was trembling, right on the razor's edge, when he finally pulled away. The loss made her cry out. Fabric rustled. Shorts hit the floor. Foil tore.

He crawled back up her body, condom in place, and kissed her deeply so she could taste herself on his tongue.

"Tell me you still want me inside you," he whispered against her lips, grinding his length against her soaked entrance—teasing, not entering.

"Stop being a tease," she panted. "I need you to fuck me, Liam. Please."

He groaned at the filthy words falling from her mouth. "That's my girl."

One slow, relentless push and he began to sink into her. Inch by inch. Stretching. Filling. Her head fell back against the pillow; his forehead dropped to hers. When he was finally seated to the hilt, they both stilled, breathing hard.

"Fuck... you feel perfect," he rasped. "So tight. So hot. Like you were made for me."

The boat rocked beneath them, and he began to move—deep, rolling strokes that dragged against every sensitive spot inside her. The pace was unhurried, devastating. Each thrust pushed a broken moan from her throat.

"Harder?" he asked, voice strained. "Or do you want me to keep teasing you until you're begging?"

"Harder," she gasped. "Please—God, Liam—"

He gave her what she asked for, hips snapping with controlled power. The bed creaked. Salt air and skin and the low slap of bodies filled the cabin. Sweat slicked their skin. His rhythm faltered as he neared the edge.

"I'm close," he warned, eyes locked on hers—dark, raw, unguarded. "Come with me, Cerys. Let me feel you fall apart around me."

She did. The orgasm crashed through her like a wave breaking against the hull—sharp, endless, stealing her breath. Not just body. Ribs. Throat. Something splitting her open from the inside.

His name tore from her lips in a shattered cry. He followed with a guttural groan, burying himself deep as his body shuddered through his own release.

Afterward, he collapsed beside her, chest heaving. She rolled into the hollow of his shoulder without thinking, fitting there like the space had been waiting for her. His arm came around her automatically, fingers tracing lazy circles down her spine.

The boat swayed gently beneath them. Outside, a halyard tapped the mast in steady rhythm. Inside, reality began its slow, unwelcome creep.

She pressed closer, breathing him in—salt, warmth, something that shouldn't feel this right. So soon. Days from now she would sail away. Back to her real life. Back to the ridiculous boyfriend pillow lying forgotten on the cabin floor.

But right now, with his heartbeat under her cheek and his warmth wrapped around her, none of that mattered.

Not yet.

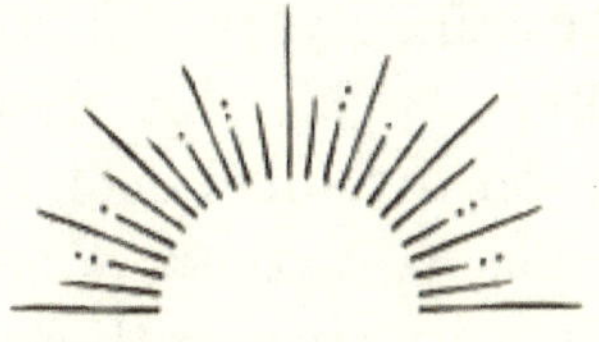

Chapter 8

Liam woke to the soft creak of the catamaran swaying in Aroha Bay, morning light filtering through the porthole and casting golden patterns across the cabin wall. For a moment, he lay still, his body warm beneath the thin sheet, acutely aware of the woman sleeping beside him.

Cerys.

Her back was to him, one arm tucked beneath the pillow, the other draped loosely over the edge of the mattress. The sheet had slipped down to her waist during the night, revealing the curve of her shoulder, her deep mahogany skin glowing in the morning light. Dark hair framed her face against the satin pillow.

He watched her breathe. The vulnerability of sleep had smoothed away the small furrow that sometimes appeared between her brows when she was thinking too hard about something.

Something in his chest tightened.

Liam had spent the night with women before. But this—waking up beside Cerys on her boat, surrounded by the evidence of her new life—felt different. The sailing books stacked up on the small desk. The worn copy of a navigation manual with sticky notes jutting from its pages. The mug with a chip in the rim sitting on the counter, probably her favorite.

He knew what it meant to leave something behind and build from scratch. Every summer he returned to Mairana Nui, the island fitting around him like an old shirt—familiar, comfortable. Every autumn he boarded a plane back to a house that felt like borrowed clothes. The difference was she'd burned her return ticket.

The boat rocked as a small wake from a passing fishing vessel rolled through the bay. Cerys stirred. Her hand moved, searching, until her fingers brushed against his arm.

Even in sleep, she reached for him—an unconscious choice that landed somewhere deeper than anything they'd done last night.

Liam propped himself up on one elbow. A loose braid had fallen across her cheek, and without thinking, he reached out and tucked it behind her ear. His fingers lingered for just a moment against the soft skin of her temple.

She'd stolen most of the blanket during the night, bunching it up against her stomach in a possessive tangle. The corner of his mouth quirked. He gave the sheet a tug, just enough to tease, and watched her nose scrunch up in sleepy protest. Her hand tightened reflexively on the fabric, pulling it closer.

Even unconscious, she was stubborn.

Outside, he could hear the sounds of Aroha Bay waking up. The distant call of seabirds. The low rumble of an outboard motor heading out for the morning catch. Somewhere on the dock, someone called out a greeting—*Mālō!*—the sound carrying across the water and settling into Liam's chest, familiar as his own heartbeat.

The boat shifted again, a little more insistently this time, and Cerys' breathing changed. Still slow, but less deep. Waking up, but not quite ready to surface. Liam stayed quiet, giving her the time. He'd learned patience early—learned that some things couldn't be rushed, that the best moments happened when you let them unfold at their own pace.

Her hand moved first, stretching out across the mattress, fingers flexing against the sheet. Then her shoulder rolled forward, and she made a small sound—half-sigh, half-hum—as she shifted onto her back. Her eyes fluttered open, still heavy with sleep, and for a heartbeat, she looked disoriented.

Then her gaze found his, and her expression softened into something that made his pulse kick up a notch.

"Morning," she murmured, her voice sleep-rough and slightly raspy. A small smile curved her lips—genuine, unguarded—and she stretched beneath the sheet like a contented cat.

"Morning." He let his hand rest on the mattress between them, close enough that their fingers almost touched.

She blinked at him slowly, hazel eyes catching the morning light, and then her smile widened just a fraction. Playful. "Did I steal the blanket?"

"Completely."

"Sorry." She didn't sound sorry at all. Her fingers found his, tangling lazily, and she gave them a gentle squeeze. "I'm a terrible bed partner."

"Didn't notice." The words came out lower than he'd intended, roughened by something he didn't want to examine too closely.

She raised one eyebrow. "Liar."

Outside, the sounds of the bay grew louder—crates being unloaded, Taviani voices bartering over fish prices. Through the porthole, Liam could see calm water reflecting pale blue morning, coconut palms swaying along the shore, and beyond that, the lush green hills rising toward the interior.

He leaned in. Their lips met, soft and lingering. Her hand came up to curl against his jaw, warm and deliberate. The kiss was unhurried, carrying none of last night's urgency.

When he pulled back, her eyes were still half-closed. He brushed his thumb across her knuckles, feeling the calluses there—line work and winch handling.

"How about breakfast?"

She nodded, pushing herself up to sit. Her dark brown twists were gloriously disheveled—loose strands escaping from what had been a neat style, fiery red highlights catching the morning light. There was a crease on her cheek from the pillow. "Sounds good."

Her eyes lit with mischief. She stretched, arching her back. "Don't forget I like my coffee strong." She snuggled back down into the sheets, pulling the stolen blanket to her chin. "Call me when breakfast is done."

Liam chuckled and shook his head. She was already closing her eyes again, burrowing into the warmth. He pressed a kiss to her forehead—salt and sun and something uniquely Cerys.

"Strong coffee. Got it."

He swung his legs off the bed, the cabin floor cool beneath his bare feet, and reached for his shorts. The fabric was slightly damp from yesterday's swim, but he pulled them on anyway. He ducked into the small head to splash water on his face, the mirror reflecting someone who looked more rested than he had any right to be.

In the galley, his hands found what they needed—coffee grounds, eggs, the pan hanging from its hook. Despite the short sleep, his body hummed with energy.

He'd made breakfast on boats before. But this—standing in Cerys' galley while she slept below, planning a morning around spending as much time around one person—felt like crossing a line he'd spent years drawing. He'd built a life around keeping things simple. Unattached. But plating scrambled eggs while warmth still clung to the sheets where she'd been, he couldn't shake the feeling that his carefully maintained balance was already shifting.

"Breakfast's ready," he called down.

Sheets rustled. Drawers opened and closed. A moment later, Cerys appeared at the bottom of the companionway, stretching in a way that made him forget what he'd been about to say. She climbed up wearing a white linen dress that moved with her, the fabric catching light against her skin.

Her smile hit him square in the chest. "Smells amazing in here. You didn't have to make all this."

"Had to make sure you're well-fed." He handed her coffee—strong, the way she'd requested—and slid into the banquette, making room for her across from him. “We should eat quickly though.”

He reached for the small bottle of hot sauce that sat amidst the array of breakfast spread.The hot sauce had a familiar label that made him grin. Pouring it generously over his eggs, he shot her a look. “Why am I not surprised you had my favorite kind?”

“It’s the only hot sauce that matters.” Cerys took the bottle from him, adding her own liberal amount. “I don’t know what I’ll do when I run out. Haven’t found it anywhere on this side of the globe.” She took a bite, then looked at him curiously. “Why the rush?”

“Market. You’re low on fresh stuff, and the Havea stall sells out fast—Nahi’s mother doesn’t mess around with her pricing, but the produce is worth it.”

“Yeah, I’ve noticed that.” Cerys finished her bite and slid out of the booth, already moving. “Then let’s go.”

They finished quickly, the comfortable silence between them punctuated only by the clink of forks against plates and the occasional appreciative hum from Cerys. Liam found himself watching her more than eating—the way she closed her eyes when she took that first sip of coffee, the small satisfied sound she made when the hot sauce hit just right, the unconscious way her foot bumped against his under the table.

When the plates were cleared, they moved through the boat with an easy rhythm. Cerys disappeared below to change while Liam rinsed dishes in the galley sink, saltwater soap making quick work of the breakfast remnants. He could hear her moving around in the cabin—drawers opening and closing, the soft rustle of fabric, a quiet curse when she stubbed her toe on something.

"You good down there?" he called, fighting back a smile.

"Perfect," she called back, her voice muffled. "Just wrestling with my camera bag."

Liam grabbed a small canvas tote from where it hung near the companionway. He filled it with essentials—water bottle, sunscreen, the cloth shopping bags Cerys kept folded in a drawer. A couple of protein bars from her galley stash. They'd be starving by the time they finished at the market.

Cerys emerged wearing coral-colored shorts and a white tank top, a loose turquoise button-down thrown over it, sleeves rolled to her elbows. Her twists were pulled back into a high ponytail, red highlights catching the morning sun. Camera bag slung crosswise over her body.

"Ready?" She caught him looking.

He held up the tote. "Yeah."

The dinghy rocked as they climbed down, Liam steadying it against the catamaran's hull while Cerys passed down her camera bag and the shopping tote. He pulled the starter cord on the outboard motor. Second try, it caught.

Less than five minutes to the main dock, cutting across calm morning water. Other boats were already moving—fishing vessels heading out, a small ferry making its way toward the outer islands, a sailboat tacking lazily across the harbor entrance. Salt and seaweed and plumeria from the shore trees.

Cerys had her camera out before they were halfway across. The way the morning light caught the water. A pair of frigatebirds soaring overhead. Colorful boats bobbing at their moorings. She worked quickly, instinctively, always seeking the next frame.

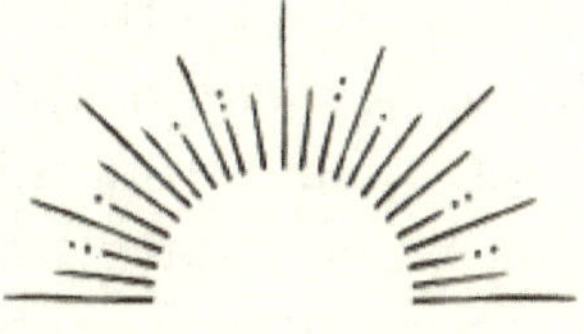

Chapter 9

Liam tied off the dinghy at the public dock, the worn cleat smooth under his calloused hands, polished by years of similar mornings. They made their way up the weathered wooden planks toward the road, passing Koa's nephew hauling a cooler of yellowfin toward the ice house, a German couple studying their phones with that lost-tourist look, and the Tavake twins racing past with dripping popsicles clutched in sticky fists—at seven in the morning, because their grandmother spoiled them rotten.

Te Rangi Market sprawled across three blocks in the heart of Aroha Bay's waterfront district, hitting them with its full sensory assault the moment they turned the corner. Canvas awnings in faded blues and sun-bleached reds stretched overhead, providing patchy shade. The air hung thick with competing scents—overripe mango sweet enough to taste, fresh-caught tuna on chipped ice, bundles of taro root still exhaling red volcanic earth, and the heavy perfume of frangipani from wooden buckets, mixed with the ever-present salt of the bay.

"*Mālō e lelei!*" voices called out as they entered the main thoroughfare. Liam responded automatically, "*Mālō!*," recognizing Sione's voice from the breadfruit stall, then Mele's higher pitch from two rows over.

Cerys moved beside him with her camera, framing shots. An elderly woman's weathered hands weaving pandanus leaves. A precarious tower of green coconuts stacked seven high. A little girl arranging hibiscus into bouquets, tongue caught between her teeth.

Vendors called out in Taviani and English, sometimes French for the yacht crowd. "*Mango teitei!* Sweet mango, three for five!" "Fresh fish, caught this morning—ask me which reef!" Machetes thudded. Flies buzzed around the fish stalls. Conversations rose and fell in three languages at once.

Cerys paused at a stall displaying woven hats, her fingers trailing over the intricate patterns.

"This one here, *keha*, it's the frigate bird pattern. For travelers, yeah? Good luck on the water." Mere's smile was warm and calculating in equal measure.

"It's beautiful." Cerys lifted the hat carefully, examining the tight weave.

"You buy, I give you good price." Mere reached for a bag.

Liam gently steered Cerys away with a hand on her lower back, leaning down to murmur near her ear. "We'll be here until sunset if you stop at every stall. Nahi's family will be sold out."

"Right, okay." She threw an apologetic smile over her shoulder at Mere, who just laughed and waved them on, already turning to her next potential customer.

They wove through the crowd, Liam navigating by instinct through the familiar maze of stalls. A little boy darted in front of them, nearly colliding with Cerys, and his mother called out an apology while pressing a slice of fresh mango into his hand to slow him down. The child stopped immediately, distracted by the fruit, and grinned up at Cerys with juice already dripping down his chin.

She laughed and crouched down to his level, pulling her camera up. "Can I take your picture?"

The boy nodded enthusiastically, striking an exaggerated pose that made his mother laugh. Cerys clicked the shutter, showed him the result on the screen, and his delighted squeal brought smiles from nearby vendors.

"*Mālō 'aupito*," the mother said warmly. "He'll talk about this all day."

They moved deeper into the market, past stalls selling taro roots stacked like small brown towers, their rough skin still caked with red volcanic soil. Next to them, bundles of taro leaves were tied with string, ready to be wrapped around fish and coconut cream for *lu pulu*. The earthy smell mixed with the sharper scent of ginger root and turmeric, piled in bright yellow and brown mounds.

Nahi's family stall occupied a prime corner spot under a faded blue awning. The display was already picked over—they'd timed it right. Wooden crates overflowed with glossy purple eggplants, thick bunches of Chinese cabbage, cherry tomatoes still on the vine, and a diminishing pile of the small, intensely sweet pineapples that only grew in Mairana Nui's volcanic soil.

Nahi's aunt Losa presided over it all, her substantial frame draped in a bright orange *puletasi*, hair pulled back in a neat bun. She spotted them and her face split wide.

"*Liam!*" Arms spread. "*Ha'u mai, ha'u mai*! And you brought our ZTube girl!"

Cerys laughed, returning the enthusiastic hug. "Hi, Losa. Your stall looks amazing as always."

"Almost empty is what it looks." Pride rang clear in her voice. "Good morning for business. But I saved some things for you, Cerys. I know you come." She reached under the table and produced a crate of vegetables—the best eggplants, a bundle of fresh herbs, several ripe tomatoes.

"You didn't have to do that."

Losa waved this off. "You make our island look beautiful on your videos. People see Mairana Nui and they want to come. Is good for everyone." She began piling produce into Cerys' arms. "These tomatoes, very sweet. And this basil—ah, you make pasta, yes? Perfect."

Liam selected pineapples with a practiced eye, checking for the right give when he pressed the bottom, the sweet smell that meant they were perfectly ripe. Mangoes next, their skin blushed with red and gold. A bunch of small finger bananas that Cerys favored for her morning smoothies.

"How much do I owe you?" Cerys already had her wallet out.

Losa named a price that was clearly discounted. Cerys countered higher. They negotiated back and forth with easy smiles.

A sharp crack split the air behind them.

A wooden crate swayed at the edge of the neighboring stall, knocked loose by a tourist struggling with too many bags. The crate tilted—

Liam caught it with both hands, steadied it against the table. Breadfruit rolled inside, their knobby green surfaces bumping against the wood. Nothing spilled.

The tourist—middle-aged, guilty expression—stammered apologies in French-accented English.

"No worries." Liam secured the crate. "Happens all the time."

The vendor, an older man named Tavita, pressed a hand to his chest. "Ai! *Mālō 'aupito*, Liam. Quick reflexes, *rāni*." He grabbed a breadfruit and thrust it into Liam's hands. "You take this, yes? For saving my stock."

"Really, you don't have to—"

"Take it. I insist. Good breadfruit, very fresh."

Liam accepted with a nod, tucking it into their shopping bag. As they finished with Losa and hefted their loaded bags, a familiar voice boomed across the market.

"*Liam!*"

His Uncle Paiwai made his way through the crowd, his broad frame cutting a path through the morning shoppers.

"*Matua kēkē*." Liam clasped his uncle's hand, accepting the brief embrace that followed—the traditional pressing of foreheads, the exchange of breath. "*Mālō e lelei.*"

"*Mālō, mālō*." Paiwai's eyes crinkled with warmth before sliding to Cerys. "*Cerys! Ha'u mai!*" He swept her into a hug that lifted her slightly off her feet, making her laugh.

"Hi, Paiwai. Good morning."

"Good morning, good morning. You feed this boy breakfast? He look too skinny to me." Paiwai poked Liam in the ribs, grinning.

"He made *me* breakfast, actually," Cerys said, and something in her tone—the easy affection, the casual intimacy—made Paiwai's eyebrows rise with interest.

"Ā *pēnei?*" Paiwai's grin widened. "My nephew, he cooks now. Very domestic."

Before Liam could respond, Anahera appeared around the edge of a produce stall, arms laden with bulging cloth bags. She was shorter than her husband, compact and energetic, with silver streaking through her dark hair and sharp eyes that missed nothing.

She took one look at them standing close together, shopping bags intermingled, and her expression shifted from surprised to delighted.

"Cerys! Liam!" She thrust her bags at Paiwai and moved forward to embrace them both. "What perfect timing. I was just telling Paiwai we should have you both over for dinner again soon." Her tone shifted, became command rather than suggestion. "Tomorrow night. You'll come."

Liam opened his mouth to deflect—he could already see where this was heading—but Cerys spoke first.

"We'd love to. What can we bring?"

"Ai, nothing. You are guests." Anahera waved this away, already planning. "I'll make *ota ika*, the way you liked last time. Maybe some *'umu* chicken if Paiwai gets the fire going early enough." She turned to Liam with a knowing look. "And something spicy for you two. I know the island food is too mild for you both."

Cerys laughed. "You know us too well."

"Tomorrow night, then. Six o'clock. Don't be late—you know how Paiwai gets when food is sitting." Anahera patted Cerys' arm, then bustled off, already calling out to another vendor.

Paiwai lingered, his expression shifting to something more serious. "It's good to see you happy, *rāni*. Your aunt worries." Then his grin returned. "Now she'll worry about feeding you both enough. Bring appetite tomorrow, yes?"

Liam hadn't realized how visible it was—the lightness he'd been carrying these past few days, the way being with Cerys had softened something in him that had been wound tight for months. He met his uncle's eyes and gave a small nod. "We will."

They watched Paiwai rejoin his wife, and only when they were out of earshot did Liam turn to Cerys, keeping his voice low.

"You've doomed us both. They're going to think we're dating."

Cerys adjusted her camera bag, not quite meeting his eyes, but he caught the small smile playing at her lips. "A tragedy. Guess we'll have to fake it convincingly."

Their eyes met, held. Something sparked between them—not playful anymore, but weighted with reality.

Liam felt his chest tighten. His aunt and uncle would start asking questions, making plans, seeing a future that couldn't exist.

Because Cerys was leaving. Eventually.

And he would leave too. In a few weeks, he'd board a plane back to America, back to his job and his parents' expectations and a life that felt more like an ill-fitting coat with every passing year.

But looking at her now—the morning sun catching the red in her hair, the ease in her posture, the way she'd handled his aunt's enthusiasm—he found himself wishing it could be different.

"Come on," Cerys said softly, breaking the moment. "Let's get this food back before everything wilts in the heat."

They walked back through the market, bags bumping between them. A group of children spotted Cerys and swarmed over, chattering in rapid Taviani about wanting to be in her next video. She crouched down, promised to film at the beach later that week if their parents agreed, and sent them off with high-fives.

By the time they reached the dinghy, the sun had climbed higher. The bay sparkled, impossibly blue. Cerys paused to capture it on camera—the boats, the shoreline, the green hills rising beyond.

"You ever get tired of taking pictures of the same view?" Liam asked as he loaded their bags.

"Never the same view." She lowered her camera to look at him. "The light's always different. The water. The clouds."

He wondered if she wasn't just talking about photography.

The ride back to Cerys' catamaran was quick. They unloaded the groceries in efficient tandem—Cerys passing bags up while Liam stored them in the galley, finding room in the small refrigerator and the nets that hung from the ceiling.

When the last bag was stowed, Cerys disappeared below deck. She emerged five minutes later in a bright yellow bikini with high-waisted bottoms and a matching top that tied at the neck, her ponytail still in place, and grabbed two snorkel masks from the storage locker.

"Quick swim before it gets too hot?" She tossed him one of the masks.

Liam caught it. He pulled off his shirt. "You read my mind."

They slipped into the water off the stern. The initial shock of cool gave way to perfect temperature. This close to shore, the bay floor was visible—sand rippled by current, patches of coral emerging like underwater gardens, schools of small fish darting between the formations.

Cerys dove first, her body cutting through the water. Liam followed, equalizing the pressure in his ears as he descended, watching her point toward a cluster of pink coral just ahead. She hovered there, weightless, her ponytail floating behind her like seaweed, and gestured for him to look closer.

A tiny octopus had wedged itself into a crevice, its skin shifting from brown to match the coral around it. Its eyes tracked them, alert but unafraid. One tentacle extended experimentally toward Cerys' outstretched finger.

Then pulled back.

They surfaced together, treading water, masks pushed up onto their foreheads.

"Did you see that?" Cerys' face was lit with wonder. "It was so small!"

"*Feke*," Liam said. "Octopus. Young one. Probably just made that coral its home."

"I wish I'd brought my underwater camera." She looked back down through the clear water, still marveling.

They drifted for a while, diving to examine whatever caught their eye—a school of sergeant major fish with black stripes, a hermit crab scuttling across sand, brain coral folded like gray matter. Underwater, the world reduced itself to breath and silence.

Eventually they floated on their backs, masks off, faces to the sky. Sun on Liam's chest, cool water at his back. Cerys' hand found his beneath the surface, fingers tangling.

They said nothing. Just suspended there, together.

When they climbed back aboard, the sun hung nearly overhead. The deck burned under their feet. Cerys grabbed towels from the storage bin and they dried off in the shade, salt crystallizing in white lines on their skin.

"I'm going to need a nap before dinner tomorrow." Cerys wrung water from her ponytail. "Your aunt's meals are no joke. Last time I ate so much I could barely move."

Liam chuckled, watching water slide down her shoulders. "She takes feeding people seriously. It's a cultural thing—hospitality through food. The more you eat, the more honored she feels."

"Then I guess we'd better skip lunch tomorrow." Cerys spread her towel over the railing. "Save room."

"Probably smart."

He moved closer, brushed a drop of water from her temple. His fingers lingered at her jaw.

She leaned into the touch. "What?"

"Nothing." Everything. "Just thinking about tomorrow."

"Nervous?"

Teasing, but genuine underneath.

"No."

Yes. Not about dinner—about what it meant. The door opening, the future taking shape in his aunt's mind. In a few weeks, he'd be gone. This would become something he'd had once, briefly, in a summer that felt like a dream.

But he didn't say that. Instead, he pulled her close, kissed the top of her head where her hair smelled like salt and sunshine, and let the moment be what it was.

Perfect. Temporary. Real enough to hurt.

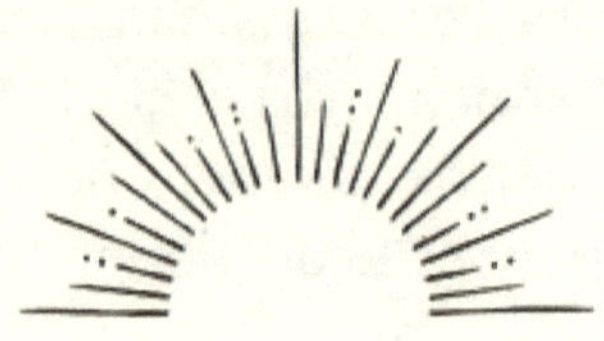

Chapter 10

Two nights later, Cerys stood in front of the small mirror mounted above her galley sink, trying to decide if she should put her hair up or leave it down. The twists fell past her shoulders, the red highlights catching the golden light of the setting sun that streamed through the porthole. She'd already changed twice—first into a coral sundress that felt too formal, then into denim shorts and a white tank top that felt too casual. Now she wore a fitted yellow tank top tucked into high-waisted linen shorts in a soft sage green, with her gold compass necklace resting against her collarbone.

She was overthinking this. It was just dinner.

Except it wasn't just dinner, and they both knew it.

Cerys left her hair down and stepped back from the mirror, taking in her bare feet against the teak flooring. When had that happened? When had shoes become optional, even for going ashore? Her feet had developed calluses in new places, had learned the texture of her deck, the coolness of early morning wood, the sun-warmed planks at midday.

Island habits, she thought, running her fingers through her hair and feeling the ever-present fine layer of salt that no amount of freshwater rinsing could completely remove. The ocean left its mark on everything here—fine salt crystals caught in the twists of her hair, the perpetual tan lines on her shoulders, even the slight warping of her journal's pages where humidity had swollen the binding.

She grabbed her small crossbody bag—phone, lip balm, the little tin of mints she'd bought at the market—and climbed up to the deck. The sun was sinking toward the horizon, painting the sky in watercolor washes of pink and orange. The air had that perfect temperature where she couldn't tell where her skin ended and the breeze began.

This was dangerous. This ease. She'd stopped thinking about her grandmother's funeral, the weight of that grief that had pressed down on her for months. Stopped obsessing over whether she had enough footage for next week's upload, stopped worrying about her family's opinions back home. The realization sent a sharp flutter through her ribcage—something between panic and relief, like surfacing after holding her breath too long. What happened when the magic wore off? When real life came calling again?

The buzz of an outboard motor interrupted her spiraling thoughts. She looked up to see Liam's dinghy cutting across the bay toward her, his silhouette backlit by the sunset. Even from a distance, she could make out the relaxed set of his shoulders, the easy way he handled the tiller.

He pulled alongside her catamaran with practiced precision, killing the motor and reaching up to grab the boarding ladder. "Permission to come aboard?"

"Denied," Cerys said, already climbing down to meet him. "I'm coming to you."

Liam raised an eyebrow but steadied the dinghy as she stepped down, his hand solid around her wrist. She settled across from him, tucking her bag between her feet.

His hair was still damp. Darker than usual, curling at the ends where it brushed his collar. He wore a soft blue linen shirt, sleeves rolled to his elbows, and khaki shorts worn to perfect softness. No shoes.

"You look nice," he said, pulling the starter cord.

The motor sputtered to life.

"Thanks." Heat rose to her cheeks. "You too."

He guided them across the bay with one hand on the tiller, the other resting on his thigh. The water was calm, barely rippling. Cerys watched the shoreline approach—houses nestled into the hillside, lights flickering on in windows, palm trees swaying against the sky. From somewhere in the village came children's laughter and the rhythmic thump of someone splitting coconuts.

Liam's place sat on the eastern edge of the village, set back from the beach with a clear view of the bay. Traditional Taviani style—open, airy, peaked roof. Soft cream paint with dark blue shutters faded to periwinkle from years of salt air. Hibiscus and plumeria crowded the small front garden, their perfume heavy on the evening breeze.

He tied the dinghy to a small dock and helped her out, his hand lingering at the small of her back as they walked up the crushed coral path.

"Fair warning," Liam said, pushing open the door. "I'm not as good a cook as my aunt."

"I'm sure it'll be great," Cerys said, stepping inside.

The interior was exactly what she would have expected, and somehow more—simple, uncluttered, but lived-in. Polished wood floors gleamed in the fading light, woven mats in deep ochre and indigo marked out the sitting area, and a low couch sat against the far wall, its faded cushions sun-bleached to a soft coral. Bookshelves lined one wall, packed tight with field guides, novels with cracked spines, and photo albums leaning at odd angles. A small kitchen opened off to the right, separated by a waist-high counter of dark wood worn smooth by years of use. The whole space smelled faintly of salt and something herbal—maybe lemongrass—and underneath it all, the warm scent of sun-baked wood.

"Make yourself at home," Liam said, already moving toward the kitchen. "Want something to drink? I've got beer, coconut water, or water water."

"Coconut water sounds perfect."

She drifted to the bookshelves while he retrieved drinks from the refrigerator, the soft thud of the door closing mixing with the distant rhythm of waves and the faint hum of evening insects starting up outside. *Field Guide to Pacific Marine Life. The Old Man and the Sea.* Several books with Taviani titles she couldn't read, their covers decorated with stylized ocean motifs. A worn copy of *Desert Solitaire* with a cracked spine. She pulled it out, flipped it open, and found margin notes in neat handwriting—questions, observations, emphatic underlines.

"Snooping already?" Liam appeared beside her with two glasses, handing her one. His proximity brought the scent of soap and clean cotton.

"Learning," Cerys corrected, taking a sip. The coconut water was cold and slightly sweet, the taste clean and bright. "You're an annotator. I respect that."

"Can't help it. If I'm not writing in a book, I'm not really reading it."

"Same." She slid the book back into place, her fingers lingering on the spine. "What are we making for dinner?"

"Something simple. *Oka i'a*—raw fish salad with coconut milk and vegetables. And rice. I picked up fresh mahi-mahi this morning."

"Can I help?"

"Absolutely." He set his glass down and moved into the kitchen, gesturing for her to follow. "You can chop vegetables. I'll handle the fish."

They fell into an easy rhythm. Liam diced the mahi-mahi into perfect cubes while Cerys worked on tomatoes, cucumbers, and bell peppers. The kitchen was small enough that they kept bumping into each other—his hip against hers when he reached for the lime juice, her elbow brushing his ribs when she turned to grab the cutting board.

The air grew thick with citrus and fresh fish. Underneath: the earthy sweetness of cilantro he'd pulled from a pot on the windowsill. Steam rose from the rice cooker.

"You know what you're doing with a knife," Liam said.

"My grandma taught me. She was very particular about knife skills." The rhythmic *thunk-thunk-thunk* of her blade punctuated her words. "She said if you couldn't dice an onion without crying, you weren't concentrating hard enough."

"Was she right?"

"Absolutely not. Onions are chemical warfare." Cerys scraped the diced vegetables into a bowl. "But I appreciated the confidence."

Liam mixed the fish with coconut milk, lime juice, and chopped herbs, then folded in her vegetables. The white fish contrasted with red tomatoes and green cucumbers, everything glistening. He covered it and set it in the refrigerator to marinate.

They ate on the small lanai overlooking the bay, cross-legged on floor cushions with their plates balanced on their knees. The coconut milk was rich without being heavy, the lime juice bright and sharp. Cerys could taste the ocean in every bite.

"This is amazing," she said, chasing a piece of fish around her plate.

"It's hard to mess up when the ingredients are this good." But he looked pleased.

They ate in comfortable silence, watching the last daylight drain from the sky. The air had cooled just enough to raise goosebumps on her arms. Beyond the village, waves crashed in steady rhythm. Stars began to emerge, tentative at first, then multiplying until the whole sky was alive with them.

From somewhere down the beach, she heard the soft strum of a ukulele and children's voices singing, the sound drifting on the breeze. A dog barked twice, then fell silent. The scent of wood smoke mingled with something herbal—lemongrass, maybe—from a neighboring cook fire.

"Do your parents ever come back here with you?" The question came out before she'd fully thought it through, but Liam didn't seem fazed.

He set his fork down, considering. "They brought me over the first time when I was eight. My dad's parents—my grandparents—were still alive then. After that, it was just me and my dad for a few summers. We'd come for a month, stay with family, and he'd take me fishing, teach me to sail, all of it." His voice softened. "But after both my grandparents passed, he stopped coming. I think it was too hard for him. Too many memories."

Cerys could picture it—a younger Liam learning to tie knots on his grandfather's boat, the old man's weathered hands guiding smaller ones. The weight of those lost summers hung in the space between them.

"I'm sorry," she said quietly.

"Yeah." Liam picked up his glass, swirled the water, and she noticed the way his jaw tightened just slightly. "He still calls Uncle Paiwai almost every day. I think he misses this part of his life more than he lets on."

"And your mom?"

His mouth quirked, not quite a smile. "My mom never really took to the island. She came that first time, did her best, but I think she was counting the days until we left. She's not outdoorsy. She likes structure, routine, air conditioning." He paused, his gaze drifting toward the darkening bay. "I don't think she understands why I keep coming back. Why I need this."

Cerys understood what he wasn't saying. The weight of being split between two worlds, two families, two versions of himself. The exhaustion of constantly translating, mediating, trying to honor both sides while losing himself in the middle.

She knew what it felt like to be caught between what you were supposed to want and what you actually needed.

"That sounds lonely," she said.

Liam looked at her then, really looked at her, and she felt the full force of his attention—warm and steady and unguarded. Something shifted in his expression, a barely perceptible softening around his eyes. "Yeah," he said, his voice dropping lower. He held her gaze a beat longer than necessary before looking down at his hands. "It is."

The moment stretched between them, heavy with understanding. A breeze stirred the palms overhead. The ukulele had stopped, replaced by the steady pulse of the ocean.

Liam stood, collecting their plates. "Come on. Let's walk down to the beach."

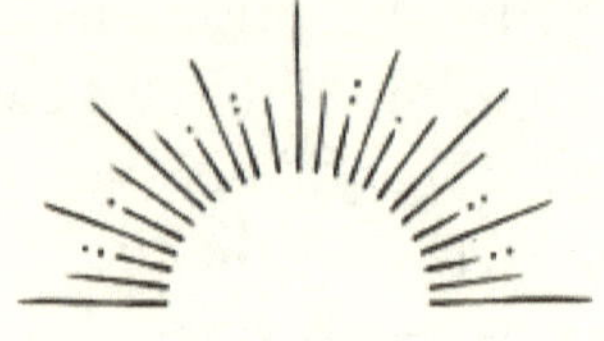

Chapter 11

They left the dishes in the sink and walked barefoot down the path to the shoreline. The sand was still warm, soft, and fine between Cerys' toes. The waves rolled in gently, barely breaking, their rhythm like breathing.

At the waterline, the sand was firm and cool. The moon was nearly full, bright enough to cast shadows, to turn the ocean silver. From somewhere up the beach came the slow melody of a ukulele and children's laughter. Night insects thrummed steadily. Palm fronds rustled overhead, sounding like rain that hadn't yet fallen.

"Tell me about your job," Cerys said. "Back in the States."

Liam bent down to pick up a piece of sea glass, turning it over before slipping it into his pocket. "I'm a park ranger. Environmental conservation specialist, technically, but mostly I just spend my days outside making sure people don't do stupid things in beautiful places."

"That sounds perfect for you."

"It is." He smiled, genuine and unguarded. "It's the closest I could get to being paid to play outside. I get to hike, monitor wildlife, teach people about the ecosystem. The pay's not great, but it's enough. And I get summers off, which means I can come here."

"Do you like it? The job, I mean. Not just the perks."

He was quiet for a moment, his gaze drifting toward the dark line where ocean met sky. "Most days, yeah. I like the work, the purpose. I like feeling like I'm protecting something that matters." He paused, his jaw tightening slightly. "But there's this part of me that wonders if I'm just going through the motions. Like I picked the safest version of the life I actually want."

"What would the unsafe version look like?"

Liam glanced at her, something vulnerable flickering across his face. He stopped walking, turned to face the bay—the dark water, the scattered lights of the village, the silhouette of the mountains against the stars. "Living here full-time. Working with my uncle on reef restoration. Teaching kids how to read the currents the way my grandfather taught me." His voice dropped lower. "Something that feels less like compromise and more like choice."

"Why don't you?"

His shoulders lifted slightly, then dropped. "Because my parents gave up everything to move to America. Because I'm supposed to build on that sacrifice, not throw it away to move backward." The words came out flat, like he'd said them so many times they'd worn smooth. "Because I'm the only kid, and if I leave, they have no one."

Cerys wanted to say something—that he deserved to live his own life, that he couldn't sacrifice his happiness for someone else's expectations, all the things she'd had to learn herself. But she knew from experience that platitudes didn't help when you were caught in that particular trap. So instead she just reached for his hand and laced her fingers through his.

His grip tightened, warm and solid.

They walked in silence, the ocean their only soundtrack. The air grew thick and humid—the kind that made everything feel closer. Cerys smelled it on the breeze: petrichor waiting to happen, salt, something green from inland vegetation.

She bent down, scooped up a handful of water, and flicked it at him.

The droplets caught him across the chest. He stopped, looked down at the wet spots, then up at her. "Did you just—"

"Maybe." She backed away, grinning.

"Oh, that was a mistake."

He closed the distance in three strides and scooped up his own handful. Cerys shrieked and dodged, but he was quicker. The water hit her shoulders—shockingly cold. She gasped, laughing, and caught him square in the face with her retaliation.

Chaos. Both of them breathless, soaked, alive. Cerys' hair dripped. Her shirt plastered to her skin. Liam's shirt went transparent, his hair wild where he'd pushed it back, and he was grinning in a way she'd never seen—completely unguarded, boyish, beautiful.

The night insects crescendoed. Palm fronds rustled overhead. The air turned electric.

She went to splash him again but he caught her wrist, pulling her toward him.

Too close. Breathing hard. The laughter died in their throats.

It happened between one breath and the next.

Liam's hand came up to cup her face, thumb brushing water from her cheek. Then he leaned in.

She rose on her toes to meet him.

The kiss started soft—tentative—but deepened almost immediately. Cerys fisted his wet shirt, pulling him closer. His arm wrapped around her waist, drawing her flush against him.

She tasted salt on his lips—ocean and sweat and something uniquely him. His fingers tangled in her hair, and she made a small sound that seemed to undo something in him.

He pulled back just enough to breathe, forehead resting against hers. "Cerys—"

She didn't let him finish. She kissed him again, harder this time, walking him backward until his legs hit the dry sand and he sat down heavily, pulling her with him. She ended up straddling his lap, volcanic sand everywhere—in her hair, under her fingernails, between her toes.

She didn't care.

His hands settled on her waist, scrunching up the wet fabric. She could feel the restraint in his touch.

Cerys pulled him closer by the collar, kissing him with everything she had. His control slipped. His grip tightened, one hand sliding up her spine to cradle the back of her head.

The insects quieted—or maybe their thrumming just couldn't compete with the rushing in her ears. The wind picked up, carrying the scent of rain and tiare flowers, and she felt the first fat drop hit her shoulder.

Warm as bathwater.

They kissed until the world narrowed to just this—mouths and hands and the full-body hum of wanti-ng someone completely.

When they finally broke apart, Cerys was shaking. Not from cold—the night was warm, the ocean warmer, the rain warmer still—but from the sheer intensity of it. From the realization that this wasn't just attraction or chemistry or a vacation fling.

This was something that could rearrange her entire life.

Liam's eyes searched hers, his chest rising and falling rapidly, his hands still anchored on her waist like he was afraid she might disappear. "We should probably talk about this," he said, his voice rough.

"Probably," Cerys agreed.

Neither of them moved.

The rain intensified suddenly—what had been a steady drizzle turned violent, fat droplets hitting Cerys' shoulder with enough force that she felt them through her wet shirt. The sky opened up completely, tropical rain falling in thick, heavy sheets that turned the world into a watercolor painting.

Cerys looked up, letting the rain hit her face, and *laughed*—bright and unrestrained, the sound bubbling up from somewhere deep in her chest. The kind of laugh she hadn't heard from herself in years, the kind that came from pure, uncomplicated joy.

"Come on!" Liam was on his feet, pulling her up with him, his hand warm and solid around hers.

They ran.

Sand grabbed at their feet. Rain plastered her hair to her skull, ran in rivulets down her neck, soaked through her already-wet clothes until she couldn't tell where ocean ended and storm began. Liam's hand was anchored in hers, pulling her forward, and she followed blindly, laughing the whole way.

Her foot caught on something—a root, a piece of driftwood—and she stumbled. Liam's arm shot out, catching her around the waist before she could hit the ground, and their momentum carried them forward until her back hit the wall of his porch with a soft *thud.*

The impact knocked the breath from her lungs—or maybe it was the way Liam stared at her, pupils blown wide, chest heaving, rainwater streaming down his face in rivulets. His hand stayed locked on her waist; the other braced the wall beside her head, caging her without touching.

For a long heartbeat, neither moved. Just the drum of rain on the overhang and the thunder of her pulse.

Then he kissed her.

Raw hunger—no preamble, no caution. Mouth crashing into hers, she met him with the same force, fingers twisting in his soaked shirt, pulling him impossibly closer. His leg slid between hers, thigh pressing firmly against her core through wet denim. She gasped into his mouth; he swallowed the sound.

His hands bracketed her hips, thumbs digging into the soft hollows above her hip bones. She rocked against his thigh instinctively, chasing pressure. He groaned low, the vibration traveling straight through her.

"Cerys." Her name came out wrecked, gravel-rough. He pulled back just enough to rest his forehead against hers, breath hot against her lips. "You shouldn't go back out in this storm."

It wasn't really a question. More like an invitation wrapped in an out.

She didn't want the out.

"I don't want to leave," she said, voice steady even as her hands shook against his chest.

Something dark and decisive flickered in his eyes. He kissed her again—slower now, but deeper, tongue sliding against hers with deliberate intent. The last thread of his restraint snapped.

They stumbled through his front door, still locked together, hands frantic, leaving wet footprints across the floor. He kicked the door shut. Rain hammered the roof like applause.

"We're soaked," she managed between kisses.

"Yeah." His fingers found the hem of her shirt, grazing bare skin at her waist. "We should fix that. Slowly."

They peeled off layers with fumbling urgency that kept dissolving into laughter. Her shirt snagged on her ponytail; he hopped on one foot trying to yank off a stubborn shoe. The absurdity only made the heat sharper.

But when her shirt finally came free and his gaze raked over her, the laughter died. His eyes darkened, tracing her like she was something sacred and filthy all at once. Hands settled on her bare waist—warm, sure.

"You're so fucking beautiful," he murmured, almost reverent, but the edge in his voice promised sin. "Been thinking about getting my hands on you like this for too long."

Her knees went weak.

She kissed the rain from his collarbone, his shoulder, the hollow of his throat. His breath hitched. Hands traced her spine—gentle but possessive, thumbs stroking the sensitive dip above her ass.

She pushed him backward until his knees hit the bed. He sat. She climbed into his lap, palms flat on his chest, feeling the thunder of his heart. His hands gripped her hips.

"Cerys." Her name like a plea. Head tipping back.

She threaded fingers through his wet hair, tilting his face up. His eyes were nearly black—vulnerable, hungry.

"I'm here," she whispered. Kissed him again.

She reached for her bra straps. He helped—slow, reverent—unclasping, sliding fabric away. Dropped it somewhere irrelevant. His gaze devoured her in the moonlight spilling through the window. No rush. Just looking.

"What?" she breathed.

"Nothing." He drew her closer. "Just trying to memorize every inch before I ruin you with my mouth."

Heat flared low in her belly. She rocked against the hard length straining his jeans. He groaned, hands sliding up to cup her breasts, thumbs circling her nipples until they ached.

"Liam—"

He hummed, then bent to take one peak into his mouth—slow licks, gentle suction, then a light scrape of teeth that made her arch. He gave the other the same torturous attention while his hands roamed lower, thumbs hooking into her waistband.

"Undress for me," she rasped.

He laid her back on cool sheets that smelled like him—ocean, wood, clean sweat. Stood at the foot of the bed and stripped deliberately, letting her watch. Belt clinked. Jeans hit the floor. He was hard, thick, ready. Her mouth went dry.

She slipped out of her underwear while he grabbed a condom from the drawer. Rolled it on with steady hands, then crawled back over her, settling between her thighs, bracing on forearms so his weight pressed just right.

He kissed her deeply while one hand slid between them, fingers tracing her slick folds—teasing circles around her clit, dipping just inside, then retreating. She whimpered.

"So wet already," he murmured against her lips. "Been thinking about how you'd feel wrapped around my fingers. Around my cock. Tell me you want it."

"I want it," she gasped. "Want you inside me. Slow. Deep. Make me feel every inch."

He groaned. Positioned himself. Pushed in slowly—inch by torturous inch—eyes locked on her face, watching every flicker of pleasure. When he was fully seated, he stilled, forehead to hers.

"Okay?"

"More than." She cupped his cheek. "Move. Please."

He did—long, rolling strokes that dragged against every sensitive spot. She wrapped legs around him, changing the angle. He groaned raw, composure fracturing.

The pace built. Bed frame creaked against the floorboards. Rain pounded harder outside. His breathing turned ragged against her neck—her name in broken pieces: "Cerys... fuck... Cerys..."

She dug nails into his back, urging him deeper. His hand slipped between them, thumb circling her clit with perfect pressure.

"I'm close," she gasped.

"Come for me," he rasped. "Let me feel you clench around my cock. Let me hear how good I make you feel."

The orgasm rolled through her—deep, endless waves that started in her core and spread to her chest, her throat. She held him tight as it crashed over her.

He followed moments later—body shuddering, face buried in her neck, a low, primal sound tearing from his throat.

They lay tangled, skin cooling, rain still drumming. His fingers traced lazy patterns on her back. She nestled closer, breathing him in.

Near the bedroom door, she could see the outline of a duffle bag half-visible in the shadows. Temporary. Transient. Just like her own life had become.

She could feel herself falling—had already fallen, maybe.

She was supposed to be just passing through. Finding herself. Building her independence. Not falling for someone who lived half a world away, someone with his own complicated life.

But lying here in the dark with Liam's heartbeat steady under her ear, his fingers drawing nonsense patterns on her skin, she recognized the feeling she'd been avoiding.

Oh no, she thought. *I'm in trouble.*

"Mmm?" His voice was rough with sleep, that deep baritone softened to barely more than a rumble in his chest. His hand paused its circling for just a moment before resuming.

"Nothing," she whispered. "Go to sleep."

He made a sound low in his throat—contentment, maybe, or something close to it. Within minutes, his breathing evened out, his chest rising and falling in the slow, steady rhythm of sleep.

Cerys lay awake longer, listening to the rain drum against the roof and his heartbeat beneath her ear. Outside, the storm continued its relentless rhythm. She should be thinking about logistics. Timelines. All the reasons this was complicated.

Instead, she closed her eyes and let herself feel the warmth of his skin against hers. The safety of his arms around her.

Tomorrow could wait.

Chapter 12

Cerys woke to gray morning light filtering through unfamiliar curtains, and the warm weight of Liam's arm draped across her waist. For a moment, she lay perfectly still, listening to his slow, even breathing against her shoulder blade, feeling the rise and fall of his chest pressed against her back. The air held that peculiar stillness that comes after storms—humid and heavy with salt, carrying the faint scent of rain-soaked earth and distant surf.

The storm had passed sometime in the night, leaving behind that distinctive quiet—the world scrubbed clean and waiting. Through the gap in the curtains, she could make out the silvered remains of puddles, and somewhere in the distance, she heard the rhythmic creak of boats rocking in their slips.

She felt Liam stir behind her, his arm tightening slightly before he pressed a kiss to her bare shoulder—soft and unhurried, like he had all the time in the world. The warmth of his mouth against her skin made her breath catch.

"Morning," he murmured against her skin, his voice rough with sleep, deeper than usual and textured like sand.

"Morning," she whispered back, turning in his arms to face him.

His hair stuck up on one side, pillow-creased and completely unguarded. The sight of him like this—rumpled and soft and *hers*, at least for this moment—made something shift in her chest.

He smiled, slow and warm, and the thought arrived with sharp clarity: *This isn't a fling. This is the kind of thing that follows you home.*

"Sleep okay?" His thumb traced lazy circles on her hip bone, calluses catching slightly against her skin.

"Better than okay." She smoothed down the worst of his bedhead, fingers lingering. "You?"

"Best I've slept in months."

They stayed tangled together in the soft morning light, talking in low voices about nothing important—favorite breakfast foods, worst sunburns, the particular sound rain makes on different roofs. The kind of conversation that was really just an excuse to stay close, to memorize the shape of each other's smiles.

Eventually, reality intruded in the form of Liam's phone buzzing insistently on the nightstand. He groaned, reaching for it without untangling himself from her completely, squinting at the screen with one eye.

"Paiwai," he said, his expression shifting from contentment to something more complicated. "He needs help at the docks."

Cerys felt the shift in his body—the way responsibility settled back over him like a familiar coat. She wanted to pull him closer, to keep this moment suspended in amber a little longer. But she understood duty. The pull of obligation that didn't wait for convenient timing.

And maybe she needed the space too. To process what last night meant. What *this* meant.

"Go," she said. "I should probably check on *New Horizons* anyway."

He looked at her for a long moment, something uncertain flickering across his face—like he was trying to read whether this was really okay, whether last night had changed something fragile between them. His thumb traced a slow circle on her hip bone, as if memorizing the shape of her.

"I'll text you when I'm free?"

"Yeah." She kissed him, quick and reassuring, trying to convey without words that she wasn't going anywhere, that this wasn't just a storm-night fluke. "Text me."

They extracted themselves from the bed with reluctance, gathering their mostly-dry clothes from the floor. Getting dressed felt strangely domestic—him handing her shirt to her, her bumping his hip with hers as they navigated the small space. The morning air held traces of last night's rain, damp and heavy with salt, mixing with the warmth of his skin and the faint scent of coconut from his soap.

When they reached his front door, Liam pulled her back for one more kiss—longer this time, thorough, his hand cupping her jaw like she was something precious.

The kind of kiss that made her forget her own name, that made her knees go liquid and her heart do complicated things in her chest.

"I'll see you later," he said against her mouth, his voice still rough with sleep and want.

"You better," she managed, and he grinned—that slow, devastating smile that made her stomach flip.

She walked back to the marina in the clear morning light, her clothes still slightly damp, her hair a disaster, and she didn't care at all. The world felt different somehow—sharper, more vivid, like someone had turned up the saturation on reality. Puddles reflected the sky in dark mirrors, and somewhere in the distance, boats shifted gently in the harbor, and seabirds called out to the fresh morning.

The concrete was still slick beneath her sandals, and when she passed the coconut bread auntie setting up her folding table for the day, the woman gave her a knowing smile that made Cerys' cheeks warm.

I'm in so much trouble, she thought again, but this time it felt less like a warning and more like a promise. Like stepping off a cliff and discovering she could fly.

• • •

By mid-morning, Cerys had showered, changed, and confirmed that *New Horizons* had weathered the storm perfectly. She'd checked her messages—one from her mother asking about the weather, one from Liam saying Paiwai had him rebuilding half the south dock, and three ZTube notifications she mostly ignored.

She texted back:

No worries. Just text when you're free. I'll probably wander around town.

His response came immediately:

Explore. I'll find you later.

With several hours to kill, Cerys set out to explore Mairana Nui properly—not as a sailor checking in at the marina, but as someone who might actually stay. The thought arrived with a flutter of something she wasn't quite ready to name.

Morning light painted the town in sharp clarity. The storm had left everything scrubbed clean—air thick with salt and minerals, puddles catching fragments of sky. Water dripped from awnings in an irregular patter. Somewhere deeper in, metal rang against metal, a scooter hummed past, children shouted.

She wandered the marina district on slick concrete. Shop windows crowded with hand-painted pottery—blues and greens in wave patterns. Woven baskets hung from doorframes, their geometric designs more intricate than she'd realized. No room for any of it on *New Horizons*, but she paused anyway.

At the commercial district's edge, fishermen mended nets in the sun. Practiced hands, fingers flying through impossible repairs. The nets stretched across weathered frames, and the men worked in silence, occasionally murmuring in Taviani.

One of the older men glanced up as she passed, face creased with decades of sun and salt. "Storm treat you well?"

"Very well." The smile that spread across her face was too revealing, too honest. She didn't care.

He grinned knowingly, crow's feet deepening, and went back to his nets.

Past the marina's tourist edge, she found the island's gentler rhythms—the parts that existed for residents, not visitors. Mothers pushed strollers, navigating puddles with practiced ease. Shop owners swept water from doorsteps, calling greetings in a mixture of English and Taviani. Yeast and butter drifted from bakery windows, mixing with frangipani sweetness.

Different from her life in North Carolina—from polished veneer and scheduled efficiency. Here, time moved at its own pace. No one rushed.

Neither was she.

At one corner, an elderly woman—*auntie*, Cerys had learned to call women of a certain age here—presided over a folding table laden with golden-brown loaves.

"Coconut bread?" The woman's smile was warm and gap-toothed. "Fresh this morning. You try."

Before Cerys could politely decline, a still-warm piece was pressed into her hand. She bit into it—sweet and dense, shredded coconut throughout and a whisper of vanilla that made her close her eyes.

"That's incredible," she said.

The woman beamed. "You come back Saturday. Pineapple-guava bread. You'll love."

"I will," Cerys promised, meaning it. The thought arrived unbidden, settling in her chest with unexpected weight: *Is this what staying feels like? Or am I just pretending this could work?*

She was still savoring the last crumbs when a familiar voice called out.

"Cerys!"

She turned to find Terry, Myles, Nadia, and Finlay approaching from a small café, paper cups in hand, looking considerably more awake than yesterday.

"Hey," Cerys said, surprised by how genuinely glad she was to see them.

"Survived the storm?" Nadia called out, her red hair pulled into a messy bun that looked deliberately artful.

"Barely," Cerys said with a grin. "You?"

"Our villa lost power for like two hours." Nadia's expression was pure tragedy. "We had to use *candles*."

Terry snorted. "You spent the whole time taking moody selfies by candlelight."

"Aesthetic content is never wasted," Nadia said primly, then her face broke into a grin. "Fancy grabbing coffee with us? There's this place down the street that does these insane flavored lattes."

"I'm good, actually." Cerys held up her now-empty hands. "Just had some coconut bread from that auntie back there."

"Oh, the one by the blue awning?" Finlay asked, adjusting his glasses. "She's brilliant. Gave us samples yesterday."

They fell into step together, drifting along the rain-slicked sidewalk—past a woman hanging laundry that snapped like flags in the breeze, past the warm yeasty smell of more baking. A motor scooter buzzed past, its driver calling out a greeting in Taviani.

Myles, predictably, started asking about her camera setup again—storm footage, upload schedules, gear reviews. She answered but found her attention snagging elsewhere: sunlight fracturing into rainbows in puddles, children's voices spilling from a nearby schoolyard, the unhurried pace of morning routines.

"So listen," Myles said eventually, adjusting the camera bag on his shoulder. "We're planning to check out Tama's band tonight. You know Tama, right? Kae's mate?"

"All locals," Finlay added. "Supposed to be really good. Island rock or something."

"You should come," Nadia said immediately, latching onto Cerys' arm. "It'll be fun. Very authentic island experience and all that."

Cerys hesitated. Part of her wanted to say yes immediately—the part that had woken up in Liam's bed this morning feeling more settled than she had in months. But another part whispered that saying yes meant something. Meant choosing *this*—this island, these people, him. Meant closing doors to other adventures, other friendships forming organically in hostels and anchorages she hadn't reached yet. The English group would leave in a week, move on to their next destination. She could too. That had always been the plan.

Except the plan was starting to feel like someone else's life.

"I don't know—" she started.

"Nope. No excuses. You're coming." Nadia squeezed her arm. "Promise me. Otherwise I'll be stuck with these three all night and Terry's already threatened to document every song on video."

"Only the good ones," Terry protested, her piercings catching the morning light.

"Promise," Nadia insisted, fixing Cerys with an exaggerated pleading look.

"Okay, okay. I promise. Where and when?"

"Around seven?" Finlay said.

"I'll be there," Cerys agreed, and meant it.

They parted ways at the next intersection—the English group heading toward some waterfall hike, Cerys continuing her aimless wandering. The invitation sat warm in her chest, mixing with the lingering glow from last night, the taste of coconut bread, the promise of music and friends later.

And beneath it all, quieter: the knowledge that every yes to Mairana Nui was a no to everywhere else. That freedom meant infinite possibilities only as long as you didn't choose one.

She pulled out her phone and texted Liam:

Got invited to Tama's show tonight. You going?

His response came a few minutes later:

Was planning on it. Want to go together?

She stared at the screen. Three words that shouldn't feel weighted. *Want to go together.* Not just tonight. Not just to the show.

She smiled at her screen, typed back:

Yeah. That would be good.

Liam

Dinner at the Beach Shack first.

Cerys

Perfect.

Cerys pocketed her phone and kept walking, the day stretching out before her with the kind of unhurried promise she was still learning to embrace. Even as she wondered how long she could hold onto it before something—or someone—asked her to decide what she really wanted.

• • •

Liam arrived at exactly six, his hair still slightly damp from a recent shower, wearing a loose linen shirt in deep blue that made his eyes look almost amber in the evening light.

"Hey," he said, his smile slow and warm as she climbed up from the cockpit.

"Hey yourself." She'd changed into a coral sundress that tied at the shoulders, her twists loose and wild around her face, small gold hoops catching the light. The way his eyes tracked over her made heat bloom in her.

"You look beautiful," he said simply, and offered his hand to help her onto the dock.

She took it, his palm warm and calloused against hers, and didn't let go as they started walking toward town. The night air wrapped around them—thick and humid, carrying the mingled scent of salt and hibiscus flowers. Overhead, the sky had deepened to indigo, punctuated by stars that seemed impossibly bright this far from city lights.

The Beach Shack emerged from the darkness ahead—a rustic open-air restaurant perched where sand met wooden planking, its Edison bulbs casting pools of amber light that made the whole structure glow like a beacon. The smell reached her first: grilled fish with garlic and lime, something coconut-sweet baking, the sharp brightness of fresh herbs. Her stomach reminded her she'd barely eaten since that coconut bread this morning.

Kae spotted them first, waving them over to a large table at the restaurant's edge where the wooden deck gave way to sand. "Took you long enough!"

Nahi was already there, along with three others Cerys recognized from around town—two women and a man, all in their early twenties, all with the easy sprawl of people who'd known each other their whole lives. They'd claimed the best spot, where the ocean breeze cut through the humid evening and the sound of waves provided a constant, rhythmic undertone to conversation.

"Cerys, you remember Nahi," Liam said, his hand warm on her lower back as he guided her toward an empty chair. "And this is Heeni, Mairana, and Waiara."

"The sailor," Heeni said, grinning as she leaned forward on her elbows. "Kae won't shut up about your boat."

"It's a *good* boat," Kae said defensively, which made everyone laugh—the kind of laughter that said this was an old argument, well-worn and comfortable.

Cerys slid into her seat, hyperaware of Liam settling beside her close enough that their shoulders brushed, that she could feel the warmth radiating from his skin in the humid night. The table was already crowded with dishes—platters of grilled mahi-mahi still glistening with lime and herbs, mounds of coconut rice fragrant with pandan, fresh papaya salad bright with chili and mint, cassava fries that filled the air with their earthy sweetness. Cold beer appeared in sweating bottles, leaving rings of condensation on the weathered wood, alongside plastic cups of something fruity and dangerously rum-heavy, each one adorned with hand-drawn palm trees.

"Dig in," Mairana said, pushing a platter toward Cerys with both hands. "You can't come to the Beach Shack and not try the fish. Nahi's uncle caught it this morning."

Cerys took a bite and had to suppress a sound of pleasure. The fish was perfectly grilled—charred at the edges, tender and flaking inside, the lime and garlic singing together in a way that made her want to close her eyes. This wasn't generic "island food."

Conversation flowed in tides—swelling with laughter, cresting, then receding into comfortable silence. Kae's hands carved the air as he described a tourist attempting to surf through a storm warning. Nahi fired back with his younger brother's doomed attempt to impress a girl by free-diving for pearls, nearly drowning in three meters of water. Heeni and Mairana picked apart the wreckage of Luka's failed proposal—something involving a rented yacht and his ex-girlfriend appearing at precisely the wrong moment.

Cerys watched more than she listened. Kae's whole body animated his stories. Mairana's hand on Heeni's arm when she laughed. The way they'd code-switch mid-sentence—English to Taviani and back—words she didn't know but understood anyway from context and laughter. Waiara reaching for cassava fries while gesturing, never quite completing either action. Decades of shared history made visible.

Liam stayed quiet beside her. But she felt his attention—how he leaned close when inside jokes got too dense, breath warm against her ear. His hand found hers under the table. Fingers laced. His thumb traced her palm, making it hard to follow conversation. When Kae teased him, she caught the ghost of a smile, saw his shoulders relax into it.

She was learning him. How he moved among his people. The subtle shifts. What belonging looked like on him.

"So how long are you staying?" Waiara asked.

Cerys hesitated. "I'm not sure yet. I'm just... seeing where things go."

"Smart," Heeni said, lifting her beer. "Plans are overrated."

"Says the woman who plans her outfits a week in advance," Mairana teased.

"That's different. Fashion requires forethought." Laughter rippled around the table—warm, familiar, the sound of years.

By the time they finished eating—plates scraped clean, the table a battlefield of empty bottles and crumpled napkins—the sun had disappeared entirely. The sky had deepened to indigo, stars beginning to pierce through like pinpricks in velvet. The group settled the bill in a flurry of cash and good-natured arguments about who'd eaten more cassava fries, then migrated next door in a loose, laughing cluster.

The bar was called *Te Mairana*—The Ocean—and it lived up to its name. The entire front was open to the beach, no walls to contain the space, just wooden floorboards giving way to sand in a gradual transition that made it impossible to tell where inside ended and outside began. Fairy lights were strung overhead in chaotic constellations, their warm glow competing with the silver moonlight spilling across the water. The bar itself was built from reclaimed driftwood, each piece worn smooth by salt and time, polished to a soft sheen that caught the light.

The bar was packed—locals in paint-splattered work clothes mixed with travelers in their vacation linen. Rum and salt hung in the air, cut with something floral climbing the support beams. Laughter punctuated the layered conversations.

A hum of anticipation moved through the crowd.

They squeezed into a standing spot near the stage—a raised platform with amps and a drum kit, microphone stands waiting. Liam's arm settled around her shoulders. Cerys leaned into him, her shoulder against his ribs.

"Tama's band is good," he murmured. "You'll like them."

The lights dimmed. Anticipation rippled through the room. Conversations dropped. Four musicians took the stage with confident ease.

"Kia ora, everyone," Tama said. "Thanks for coming out tonight. We're going to play some music, you're going to drink too much, and we're all going to pretend tomorrow doesn't exist. Sound good?"

The crowd roared approval, and Tama grinned—counted off with a sharp nod—"One, two, three,"—and the first chord hit like a wave breaking.

The music detonated through the space.

Island rock with a pop sensibility that felt both familiar and foreign—guitars that shimmered and growled, drums that punched through Cerys' sternum and rattled her ribs. The bass line was a living thing, relentless and infectious, thrumming up through the floorboards and into her bones. Tama's voice had a raw, unpolished edge that raised goosebumps along her arms—the kind of sound you couldn't get from a streaming app or satellite radio. This was *live*. Untamed. The way music used to feel back in college when she'd crowd into tiny venues to hear bands on the edge of breaking through, when every note felt urgent and unrepeatable.

Around them, bodies surged—swaying, leaping, drinks threatening to spill, arms flung skyward in surrender. The energy was untethered and electric, the kind of collective abandon that only crystallized when the music hit this hard and the night felt infinite and everyone understood they were living inside something that would never repeat itself exactly this way again. Cerys felt it pouring through her, reverberating in her chest, like the island itself had a heartbeat and she'd finally synced to its tempo.

Liam's arm shifted from the back of her chair to her shoulders, pulling her against his side. She leaned into him without thinking, her head finding the curve where his shoulder met his chest. His thumb traced slow patterns on her bare arm—so light it might have been unconscious, but it anchored her here, to this moment, to him.

The song shifted mid-set—something slower, dreamier. The drums softened to a heartbeat pulse, and the lead guitar picked out a melody that drifted through the humid air. Around them, the chaos gentled. People stopped dancing and started swaying, couples pulling closer, the frenetic energy settling into something intimate and hushed. Maybe the fairy lights dimmed, or maybe the world had just narrowed.

Cerys felt Liam's body angle toward her.

"Dance with me."

Not a question.

A bright voice cut through the moment like a firecracker popping in still air.

"Hi! I'm Paiti. I know everything about everyone. What's your name?"

Cerys blinked and found herself face-to-face with a girl who couldn't have been more than nineteen, with wild curly hair pulled into a high ponytail, warm brown skin, and eyes that sparkled with the kind of mischief that promised either delight or disaster. She wore a crop top covered in hibiscus flowers and denim shorts, and she'd planted herself directly in front of Cerys with the confidence of someone who'd never met a stranger.

"Uh—Cerys," she managed.

"Can you *not* scare off the tourists?" Kae called from somewhere behind them, laughing.

Liam sighed, but there was affection in it. "Cerys, this is our cousin Paiti. Paiti Taneti. Paiti, this is Cerys."

Paiti ignored him completely, her attention laser-focused on Cerys. "Are you staying long?"

"I'm—not sure yet—"

"Do you like diving? Because if you like diving, Liam can take you. He knows all the best spots. He won't tell you that, but he does."

"Paiti—" Liam started, but she was already barreling forward.

"Do you know he cooks when he's anxious?" Paiti leaned in conspiratorially, her voice dropping to a stage whisper that absolutely everyone nearby could hear. "So if he starts feeding you too much, he likes you."

The entire group erupted. Kae doubled over laughing, Nahi nearly spilled his beer, and even Heeni—who'd been mid-conversation with someone else—turned around with a delighted grin.

Cerys felt heat flood her face, a mix of secondhand embarrassment and something mortifyingly close to pleasure. She didn't dare look at Liam.

"I'm adopting you out to another family," Liam muttered.

Paiti beamed, utterly unbothered. "You love me."

"Debatable."

Cerys couldn't help it—she laughed, genuine and warm. "It's nice to meet you, Paiti."

Paiti's grin widened impossibly further. "Oh, I *like* you. You can stay."

"Thanks," Cerys said dryly. "I was worried."

"You should be. I have *opinions*." Paiti tilted her head, studying Cerys with unnerving intensity. "But you're good. I can tell."

Before Cerys could figure out how to respond to that, Liam wrapped his hand around her wrist—gentle but deliberate—and tugged her away from his cousin.

"We're dancing now," he said firmly, pulling her toward a clearer section of the floor as Paiti's laughter followed them.

"You're welcome!" Paiti called after them. "I'm *helping!*"

"Ignore her," Liam said, but he was almost smiling, that soft quirk at the corner of his mouth that Cerys was learning meant he was more amused than annoyed.

"She's sweet," Cerys said.

"She's a menace."

The music washed over them as they found their space—not quite on the makeshift dance floor, but close enough that the floorboards vibrated beneath their feet with each bass note. Liam's hand settled on her lower back, warm through the thin fabric of her dress, his palm spreading wide as if anchoring her. His other hand caught hers, fingers threading loosely between hers, thumb resting against her pulse point. Cerys let her free hand rest on his shoulder, feeling the solid warmth of him beneath the linen, the shift of muscle as he drew her closer.

They swayed together, finding an easy rhythm that had nothing to do with practiced steps and everything to do with simply moving in sync. The fairy lights cast everything in soft gold, throwing long shadows that danced across the weathered floorboards. The music seemed to wrap around them like a living thing—Tama's voice rough and tender, singing something in Taviani that Cerys didn't understand but *felt* anyway, each note reverberating through her chest like a second heartbeat. Raw. Untamed. Nothing like the polished tracks on her satellite radio or the algorithm-curated playlists she'd grown used to.

Her head found its way to the space near his shoulder, close enough that she could catch the scent of him—salt and something clean and warm that was just *Liam*. Around them, other couples swayed and the music drifted, but it all felt distant—like the rest of the world had been turned down to a gentle hum, like they were moving inside their own private constellation.

I don't want this to end, Cerys thought, and the realization hit her with unexpected force—a bright ache lodging somewhere beneath her sternum. Not just the dancing, not just the night. All of it. The island, the easy mornings and golden afternoons, the way Liam looked at her. The way she felt when she was with him. The way he moved through his world with such quiet confidence, so rooted in this place and these people, and how he'd opened a space for her in it without hesitation.

Her time with Liam. However long that turned out to be.

The thought settled into her bones like an anchor she didn't know whether to resist or surrender to.

Liam shifted, his forehead coming down to rest against hers. His eyes were half-closed, his expression soft in a way she'd never seen before—all the careful guardedness stripped away, leaving something raw and honest beneath. This close, she could count his eyelashes, could see the exact way the fairy lights reflected in his dark eyes, could feel the warmth of his exhale against her lips.

"You okay?" he murmured, his voice a low rumble she felt as much as heard, vibrating through the places where their bodies pressed together.

"Yeah." Her voice came out softer than intended, almost breathless. "Really okay."

His mouth curved, a small private smile just for her. "Good."

They stayed like that—foreheads pressed together, swaying slowly, the music building and breaking around them like waves—until Kae's voice cut through the bubble.

"Get a room!"

Liam didn't pull away immediately. Instead, he huffed a quiet laugh against her skin, his breath warm on her temple. "My family is the worst."

"They're perfect," Cerys said, and meant it.

But eventually the song ended, bleeding into something faster and more energetic, and the moment broke naturally. The group reformed around them—Kae dragging Nahi toward the bar for another round, Heeni and Mairana debating whether to call it a night, Paiti bouncing between conversations with the manic energy of someone running on pure joy and coconut water.

Liam's hand found the small of Cerys' back again, warm and grounding. "Want to get out of here?"

"Yeah," she said, relief and anticipation mixing in her chest.

They said their goodbyes—a chorus of teasing and promises to do this again soon—and slipped out into the night. The air outside felt cooler after the press of bodies in the bar, though the humidity still clung to her skin like a second layer.

They walked in comfortable silence down the sandy path, fairy lights from neighboring bars and restaurants casting golden pools on the ground. Cerys could still feel the music thrumming faintly in her bones, the ghost of Liam's hand on her back, the way his breath had felt against her temple during their dance.

Her phone buzzed—a message from Nadia in the group chat they'd apparently been added to:

That was ADORABLE. You two are killing me.

Terry:

Seriously. Get married already.

Paiti

Because of course Paiti was in the chat now.

I TOLD YOU. He cooks when he's anxious!!!

SALTWATER BETWEEN US

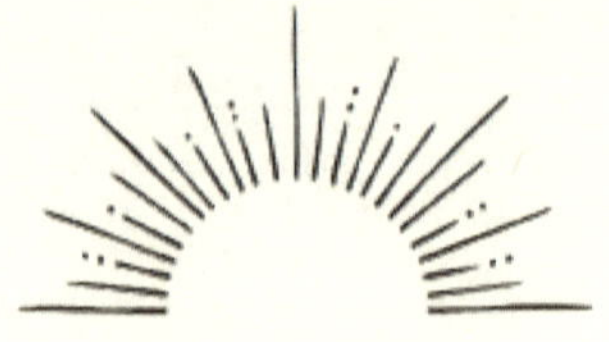

Chapter 13

The walk back to the marina was quieter than the walk to the bar had been. Not uncomfortable—just weighted with something Liam couldn't quite name. Behind them, fairy lights and laughter dissolved into darkness. Their footsteps fell soft against worn wood, the only sound between them the distant percussion of waves against the reef and the whisper of palm fronds overhead. The night air clung to his skin like a second layer, thick and warm, carrying salt and the ghost of music still thrumming in his chest.

Cerys' boat sat anchored in Aroha Bay, her twin hulls gleaming white under the moonlight. The water was glass-smooth tonight, barely a ripple disturbing the reflected stars. Around them, a handful of fishing boats bobbed at anchor, their running lights creating soft halos in the darkness. The scent of *tiare* flowers drifted across the water, mixing with salt and the faint diesel smell from the day's boat traffic.

Liam helped her into the dinghy without a word, his hand steady on her elbow as she stepped down. The small boat rocked beneath their weight, water lapping softly against the rubber hull. They made the short trip across the dark water in companionable silence, the outboard motor's purr the only sound between them.

When they climbed aboard, Cerys moved automatically to the cockpit, pulling out cushions and settling into the seating area. The solar lights she'd strung along the boom cast everything in soft amber, creating a warm pocket of illumination against the vast darkness of sea and sky. Liam settled beside her, feeling the slight give of the cushions.

"Want something to drink?" she asked, already halfway to standing.

"I'm good." Liam caught her hand gently, tugging her back down. "Just... sit with me for a minute?"

She settled beside him, close enough that their shoulders brushed. The night air was warm and salt-sweet, carrying the distant sound of waves against the reef and the occasional call of night birds from the shore. Above them, the stars were impossibly bright—the kind of sky that only existed far from city lights. The Milky Way stretched overhead like a river of light, exactly as it looked from his grandfather's favorite fishing spot on the north side of the island.

Liam let the silence stretch, his thumb tracing absent patterns against her knuckles. He'd been thinking about this all night—through the laughter and music, through dancing with her in his arms, through watching her fit so naturally into his world that it made his chest ache. The boat rocked gently beneath them, a soothing rhythm he'd known his entire life. Somewhere across the bay, he heard the soft splash of something breaking the surface—a fish or maybe a reef turtle coming up for air.

"I'm not really ready to say goodbye," he said finally, his voice quiet and rough.

Cerys turned to him, and even in the dim light he could see the warmth in her eyes, the soft curve of her smile. "Well," she said, a flirtatious note threading through her voice as she shifted closer, "who said you have to say goodbye yet?"

Her hand came up to his chest, fingers curling into the fabric of his shirt as she leaned in. The invitation was clear—come below deck, stay longer, push this goodbye further into the future. He could feel her breath against his jaw, warm and sweet.

He wanted to. Badly. The invitation in her eyes, the warmth of her hand curled into his shirt, the promise of pushing this goodbye further into some distant future—it all pulled at him with an almost physical force.

Liam caught her hand gently, stopping her. "Cerys, wait."

She paused, confusion flickering across her face. "What's wrong?"

"Nothing's wrong." He kept hold of her hand. The boat rocked gently beneath them, and he could hear the soft creak of the hull settling, the distant splash of something breaking the surface out in the bay. "I just... I need to say something first."

The air between them shifted—anticipation collapsing into something heavier. Cerys straightened, her breath catching as she read something in his expression that made her pulse stutter. The night breeze whispered across the water, carrying salt and *tiare* flowers, making the solar lights sway and cast shifting shadows that played across her suddenly uncertain face.

Liam inhaled slowly, his chest expanding as thoughts he'd been circling for days finally coalesced into words. "I understand the call of adventure," he said, his voice dropping lower, rougher. "But America has its own adventures waiting. New journeys we could take together." He paused, his dark eyes holding hers with an intensity that made the world narrow to just the two of them. "Come back with me, Cerys."

His heart hammered against his ribs. The silence stretched between them like the dark water surrounding her boat, vast and fathomless.

Cerys went completely still—that frozen quality of someone who'd just had the ground shift beneath their feet. Her fingers went slack in his grip. Her lips parted slightly, as if to speak, but no sound came. In the amber light, he watched her pupils dilate, watched the rapid flutter of her pulse at her throat.

"Cerys—"

"You want me to..." Her voice came out barely above a whisper. She swallowed hard, the movement visible. "Come back to America. With you."

"Yeah." The word came out rougher than he intended, scraping past the tightness in his chest. His thumb traced over her knuckles—once, twice—seeking purchase in the familiar gesture. "You don't have to answer right now. Just... think about it."

She stared at him like he'd just asked her to solve an impossible equation—variables that refused to align no matter how she rearranged them.

"I know what I'm asking." His voice came out rough, each word scraping past the tightness in his throat. "And I know it's not fair. But this—" he gestured between them, the space charged with everything unspoken, "—this isn't just some island fling. You know that."

Something unlocked in her. Cerys blinked. Her throat worked as she swallowed hard. Her chest rose and fell with a shaky breath that seemed to take everything she had. Her free hand found the edge of the cockpit seating, knuckles pronounced as she gripped it like an anchor. "You're right. It's not." She whispered. "It's so much more than that."

"I'm not ready to say goodbye to you either, Liam." Her voice fractured on his name. "But..." She pulled her hand free from his grip, the loss of contact immediate and visceral. She stood abruptly, moving to the rail as if distance might give her clarity. Her back turned to him now, her silhouette a dark shape against the darker water, broken only by the distant pinpricks of shore lights. "When I started this journey, I made a promise. To myself. To my grandma." Her shoulders drew up, defensive. "To see it through. To see as many shores as I could reach, to collect as many adventures as one lifetime would hold."

Liam stood, his body moving before his mind caught up. He closed the distance between them but stopped just short of touching her. Close enough to see the rigid line of her spine, the death grip on the rail, the slight tremor in her shoulders.

The breeze shifted—cooler now, almost a warning. It carried the sharp mineral scent of the reef and the distant percussion of waves breaking against the outer barrier, nature's metronome marking time they didn't have.

"And I just..." Cerys turned to face him, and the sight of her face in the amber glow knocked the breath from his lungs. Her eyes were bright with moisture that caught the solar lights, transforming them into fractured amber and gold. Pain and longing written in equal measure across her features. "Why can't you come with me?"

The question landed like a physical blow—straight to the center of his chest, stealing air and equilibrium in one devastating strike.

Around them, the night held its breath. Even the water seemed to still, the gentle lapping against the hulls falling silent as if the ocean itself waited for his answer.

"The boat is big enough for two." The words came faster now, almost desperate. Her hands gestured between them, then out toward the dark expanse of ocean. "You weren't meant to waste away in a soulless job, Liam. You could—we could—just sail. See the world together. You love the ocean, you love adventure, why would you want to go back to—"

"Waste away?" Something hot flared in his chest. "You think that's what I'm doing? Wasting away?"

Cerys blinked, taken aback by the edge in his voice.

"You might have felt that way about your job," Liam said, his voice low and controlled. "But you shouldn't put that label on me." The humidity clung to his skin. "My father worked *hard* so I could have the life I chose. So I could have options. A career. Stability." He held her gaze. "He gave up everything so I wouldn't have to choose between two worlds the way he did. And I want to share that life with you."

"But that's just it—" Cerys' voice cracked. "It sounds like you're asking me to give up everything I've only just found. A gilded cage is still a cage."

The words hung between them, heavy and damaging.

Her hand flew to her mouth almost immediately. "I didn't—Liam, I didn't mean it like that."

He stood frozen for a moment, the accusation settling over him like cold water. As if asking her to build a life with him meant asking her to surrender her own. The boat tugged gently at its anchor, responding to some subtle current he couldn't see but could feel in his bones—the ocean's restless movement, always shifting, never still.

But he could see the regret written all over her face, the way her shoulders had hunched in on themselves, the way she'd wrapped her arms around her middle like she was trying to hold something in.

Liam reached for her, wrapping his arms around her and pulling her close. She came willingly, her arms sliding around his waist and holding tight. He could feel her trembling slightly against him, could feel the rapid beat of her heart against his chest, the warmth of her breath through his shirt.

"We would still travel," he said quietly, his chin resting on top of her head. The scent of salt and *tiare* flowers clung to her hair. "Anywhere you wanted. I promise you that. But I can't just leave everything behind, Cerys. My job, my responsibilities—they're not a cage. They're the foundation my father built so I could stand on solid ground. So I could choose my life instead of having it chosen for me." He pulled back just enough to look at her, his hands gentle on her shoulders. "And I'm choosing you. I want to build something with you. Not instead of adventure—*with* it."

His eyes held hers, steady and sincere despite the ache spreading through his chest. "With you, Cerys. Not keeping you from anything. *With* you."

Cerys stayed quiet, her arms still wrapped around his waist. He felt the rise and fall of her breathing against him. The water lapped softly against the hulls.

Somewhere in the darkness beyond the boat, a night bird called—low and mournful.

The breeze picked up. Salt and reef minerals, cooler now against his skin. The solar lights overhead swayed on their hooks, casting shifting patterns across the deck.

Finally, she shook her head. When she looked up at him, her eyes were wet with unshed tears, catching the amber glow.

"Liam, I can't..." Her voice came softly. "I can't go back with you."

The words landed between them with devastating finality.

"Just think about it, Cerys." His voice remained steady even as everything inside him felt like it was breaking apart. "Please."

She nodded against his chest, but he could feel every bit of tension in her body. The way she was holding herself together through sheer force of will.

He cupped her face in his hands, tilting her head up to meet his gaze. Her dark eyes were bright with tears, her expression raw and open in a way that made something in his chest tighten painfully.

He kissed her.

Soft at first—a tentative brush of lips that deepened into something achingly deliberate. Nothing like the fierce hunger of the night before. This was slower, more devastating. A question pressed into her mouth, an answer given in the way her breath hitched, a goodbye that tasted of salt and regret. Her fingers twisted in his shirt, holding on like she could anchor this moment against the tide of what came next.

When they broke apart, the silence between them felt vast. Only the water spoke—gentle laps against the hulls, the soft groan of the boat shifting on its anchor line, their ragged breathing tangling in the humid night.

They held each other in the amber glow of the solar lights, neither moving, neither speaking. The warm breeze stirred her hair against his neck. Above them, stars scattered across the darkness like thrown salt, indifferent and eternal.

Eventually, he stepped back.

He had to. If he stayed any longer, he'd either say something he'd regret or stay until morning trying to convince her of something she clearly wasn't ready for.

"Pō *mārie*, Cerys," he said finally, the Taviani words for goodnight feeling more natural than English in this moment.

She didn't answer. Just watched him with those luminous eyes as he turned away and climbed down into the dinghy.

His hands found the familiar worn texture of the rope, the smooth fiberglass of the small boat's hull. The engine started—a low purr that seemed too loud in the quiet marina. He began the short trip back to shore.

He looked back once.

She was still standing there in the cockpit, illuminated by the soft amber glow of the solar lights, framed against the night sky and the dark silhouette of the island beyond. Watching him. One hand pressed against her chest like she was trying to hold something in. The breeze lifted her hair, and for a moment she looked like she had that first day—untouchable, luminous, impossibly beautiful.

Liam turned back to the water. Navigated toward the dock, the dinghy's wake spreading silver in the moonlight.

The humid air clung to his skin as he tied off the dinghy and stepped onto the wooden dock.

Maybe she would consider what he'd said. Maybe, somehow, she would choose to continue their adventure together. Find a way to bridge the gap between his world and hers.

But as he walked up the beach toward the path that would take him home, his feet sinking into the still-warm sand, he couldn't shake the feeling that he already knew her answer.

• • •

The next morning, Liam found himself back at the north side of the island—the bay where he'd first met Cerys. Surfboard under his arm, the sand still cool beneath his bare feet despite the climbing sun. The familiar scent of salt and reef minerals hung thick in the humid air, mixing with the sweet perfume of *tiare* flowers from the jungle edge.

He'd thought she was a goddess that day. Some mountain spirit come to life. Beautiful. Untouchable. And he'd reached for her anyway.

What the hell had he been thinking?

The waves called to him, their rhythmic crash against the reef a sound he'd known his entire life. He waded in, letting the cool water rise around his calves, then his thighs, the temperature shock clearing his head for a brief moment. Out here, he could breathe. Each wave he caught gave him a few seconds where nothing else mattered—just the curl of water, the shift of his weight, the temporary freedom of motion. The ocean stripped everything else away, left him with only muscle memory and instinct.

He rode until his arms burned and his shoulders ached, letting the physical exhaustion drown out what it could.

On his last wave in, Kae was waiting on the beach, standing in the shade of a leaning palm. The morning sun was already fierce, and sweat beaded on his cousin's forehead.

"*Kāne*, you alright?" His cousin clapped him on the shoulder as Liam trudged up the sand, board tucked under one arm.

Liam nodded, but they both knew it was a lie. The tension in his jaw gave him away.

Kae sighed, his expression softening with understanding. "*Tamai kui* Ariki always said you were too much like your Pāpā." He paused, watching Liam's face. "She knocked you off your feet. Just admit it."

Liam let out a heavy breath, dropping his board into the sand and running a hand through his wet hair. Salt water dripped down his back. "Yeah. She did." He forced his eyes to the horizon, where the morning haze blurred the line between sea and sky. "But I'll be alright."

"So you're staying?" Kae asked, hopeful. "With her? You're not going back?"

"No." The word came out flat, final. Liam felt it settle in his chest like a stone. "I asked her to come with me. She wanted me to go with her." He paused, his jaw working. The breeze picked up, carrying the distant sound of morning fishermen calling to each other across the bay. "But I can't just leave. Everything Pāpā built—it was so I could have a choice. A foundation." He held Kae's gaze. "I owe him that."

It wasn't about the job. It was about honoring what his father had sacrificed. About not letting that gift become meaningless.

Kae shrugged, a slight smile tugging at his lips despite the situation. "I don't know, man. Seems simple to me. She's beautiful, smart, funny. I'm jealous she picked you." He nudged Liam's shoulder. "If she'd asked *me* to go, my bags would've been packed before she finished the sentence."

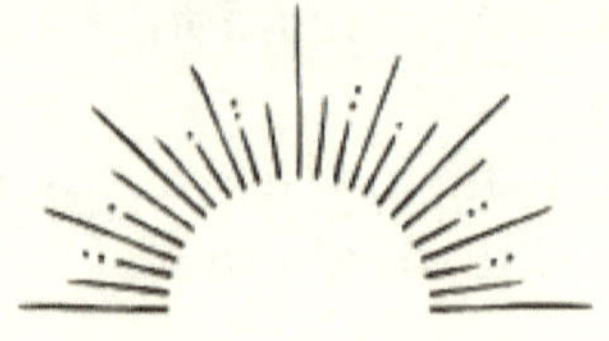

Chapter 14

Cerys sat on the deck of her catamaran, bare feet against the warm fiberglass, coffee mug cradled in both hands. The sunrise painted the sky in shades of pink and orange, the light catching on the gentle swells of the bay. The beauty of it should have filled her with peace. This was everything she'd sailed across an ocean to find. Instead, her chest ached with a tangle of heartbreak and frustration.

How could Liam expect her to give up all of this? The freedom of waking without an alarm, deciding her route over morning coffee, solving problems with her own two hands. The life she'd only just begun to claim as her own. He talked about his job in America like it mattered, like it was something worth preserving, but she'd seen the way he came alive out here—trekking through jungle trails with mud on his boots, diving into coral reefs with that look of pure wonder, standing on the deck of her boat with salt spray in his face and the wind in his hair. *That* was the real Liam, not whatever "safe" version of himself he was trying to preserve.

Of course a man would expect me to give up my dreams to be with him.

The thought arrived bitter and automatic—a reflex born from years of compromise she'd barely noticed accumulating. But even as it formed, she knew it wasn't fair. Liam had never asked her to be smaller. Never tried to reshape her into something more convenient. He genuinely believed they could build something together.

But that didn't change the core problem: she'd spent too many years bending. She wasn't going back to that. Not even for him.

Her heart had done a stupid, traitorous flip when he'd asked her to stay. Why couldn't he just come with her? The boat was big enough. They could sail to Fiji, to Vanuatu, to wherever the wind took them. But he had responsibilities. A legacy to honor.

She sighed and went inside.

Her laptop sat open on the small galley table, cursor blinking. The cabin smelled faintly of coffee and the sea. She had a blog post to write—her audience was waiting—but every time she tried to start, the words tangled.

Finally, she just started typing.

She wrote about the island. The crystal-clear water and hidden waterfalls. The way the jungle smelled after rain—like earth, green growth, and something wild. The people she'd met, their warmth and generosity.

When she got to Liam, her fingers slowed.

She wrote about their first meeting—how he'd looked at her like she was something extraordinary. About their dives and hikes. The nights they'd spent together, the heat and tenderness of it all, the way he'd held her like she was both precious and powerful.

But when she tried to write about the choice in front of her, her hands stilled.

Leaving him felt impossible. Giving up her journey felt worse.

She closed the laptop with more force than necessary and went back outside.

The sunlight danced on the water, brilliant and relentless. She picked up her camera—the familiar weight of it settling in her hands like an anchor—and focused through the lens on the shoreline, the palms, the curve of the bay. The viewfinder framed it all in neat rectangles, containable, but she knew better now. Whatever decision she made, she'd carry this place with her. The salt smell. The way the deck felt under her bare feet at dawn. And him.

Always him.

Three days passed in restless silence.

Cerys kept moving—paddleboarding at dawn through water so clear she could see her shadow on the sandy bottom, hiking jungle trails that left red mud caked on her legs, shooting footage she didn't have the heart to edit. The memory card filled with golden hours and turquoise water, with close-ups of hibiscus and wide shots of the bay, all of it technically perfect and emotionally unwatchable. She told herself she was documenting the island, but really she was just trying to outrun the ache in her chest.

It didn't work. Every sunset reminded her of Liam—the way he'd stood beside her in the cockpit, solid and unhurried, like he had all the time in the world. Every wave breaking on the reef sounded like his voice, that low rumble that made even simple observations feel weighted with meaning.

She missed him with a ferocity that surprised her. Not just the physical presence of him—though she missed that too, the warmth of his chest against her back, the way his hands steadied her on uneven ground—but the *space* he created. His steadiness. The quiet confidence in how he moved through the world, never rushing, never performing.

Missing him didn't change the fundamental problem: he wanted her to fold her life into his, and she'd only just learned how to unfold.

She'd give up the life she'd fought for. Morning coffee in the cockpit, deciding which way to point the bow. The bilge pump she'd fixed at sea with nothing but her toolkit and stubbornness.

On the fourth evening, she was updating her blog—trying to find words that didn't sound hollow—when she heard the familiar purr of a dinghy engine cutting across the bay.

Her heart kicked against her ribs. She knew that sound. Knew the rhythm of his approach.

Liam climbed aboard without asking permission, moving with that easy grace she'd memorized without meaning to—hand on the lifeline, weight shifting smoothly from dinghy to deck. He looked tired. Shadows under his eyes. Tension in his shoulders that hadn't been there before. But his smile was warm when their eyes met, and something in her chest cracked open.

"Hey," he said quietly.

"Hey."

For a long moment, they just looked at each other. The evening breeze carried the scent of salt and hibiscus across the deck. Cerys wanted to say something—anything—but the words tangled in her throat.

"Can I sit?" Liam asked, gesturing toward the cockpit.

She nodded, not trusting her voice.

They settled into the cockpit as the sky bled orange and pink, the fiberglass still warm from the day's sun beneath her thighs. The rigging clinked softly in the evening breeze. Somewhere across the bay, she could hear children laughing, the sound carrying clear across the water.

Liam sat with his forearms resting on his knees, hands clasped loosely between them. He stared out at the water, jaw working slightly. Cerys watched the dying light play across his profile—the strong line of his nose, the slight furrow between his brows.

"I've been thinking," he said finally, his voice low.

"Yeah?"

"About what I said. About asking you to stay." He turned to look at her, and the vulnerability in his eyes nearly undid her. "I don't think I said it right."

Her pulse quickened, a sharp flutter beneath her collarbone. She forced herself to stay still, to listen.

"I didn't mean to make it sound like..." He paused, searching for words. "Like you'd just be fitting into my life. That's not what I want."

"What do you want?" The question came out barely above a whisper.

Liam was quiet for a moment, his gaze drifting back to the horizon where the sun was sinking lower, painting the water in shades of copper and gold. "I want to know what happens next with us. I want more time. More conversations. More mornings waking up next to you." He ran a hand through his hair, and she caught the slight tremor in it. "But I can see now that asking you to give up all this—" he gestured at the boat, the bay, the vast open water beyond "—that's not fair."

The silence stretched between them, heavy with everything unsaid. A fish jumped somewhere nearby, the splash followed by expanding rings on the water's surface.

"I've been thinking too," Cerys said, her voice catching slightly. She looked down at her hands, then forced herself to meet his eyes. "Every day. Every hour, really."

Liam shifted closer, not quite touching her but near enough that she could feel the warmth radiating from him. "And?"

"And I'm terrified," she admitted. "Of making the wrong choice. Of losing you. Of losing myself." She swallowed hard, her throat tight. "I spent so many years making myself smaller, Liam. Safer. More convenient for other people. And I promised myself I wouldn't do that again."

"I know."

"Do you?" The words came out sharper than she intended. She took a breath, trying to steady herself. "Because what you're asking—coming back to America with you, building a life there—that feels like going backward. Like stepping back into a cage, even if it's a nicer one."

She watched something flicker across his face—hurt, maybe, or understanding. He was quiet for a long moment, his jaw working.

"That's not what I want for you," he said finally, his voice rough.

"I know that too." And she did. A tear escaped, tracking down her cheek. "That's what makes this so hard."

"You've made a decision, haven't you?" Liam asked quietly.

Cerys' throat tightened. She'd thought about nothing else. The question had circled through her head during every paddle stroke, every step up jungle trails, every moment she'd tried to lose herself in the viewfinder. She'd imagined it—waking up in his house, learning the rhythms of his life, meeting his colleagues and friends. Building something together.

And every time, she felt the walls closing in.

"I have," she said, her voice shaking. "And Liam, I can't. I can't go back with you."

She watched something break behind his eyes. He absorbed the blow with that quiet strength that made her want to take it all back, to tell him she'd changed her mind, that she'd follow him anywhere.

But she couldn't.

"I know what you're building matters," she continued, the words tumbling out now. "I know your father's legacy is important. And I know you think I could be part of it. But I just got here, Liam. I just started *living.*" She gestured around them—at the boat, the bay, the darkening sky. "This freedom—it's everything. And if I follow you now, I'm afraid I'll lose myself again."

She paused, drawing a shaky breath. The rigging clinked softly above them—small, familiar sounds that had become the soundtrack of her freedom.

"And if I follow you now..." She breathed deeply before continuing. "I'm afraid I'll lose myself again. That I'll wake up one day and realize I've traded one anchor for another—except this time, I'll be the one who chose to drop it."

Liam reached for her hand, and she let him take it.

"Okay," he said finally. Just that one word, but it carried the weight of acceptance. Of letting go.

They sat in silence as the last sliver of sun disappeared below the horizon. The sky was awash in deep purples and indigos now, the first stars beginning to appear.

"If you ever change your mind," Liam said quietly, "if you ever need a place to drop anchor for a while—I know a guy with lots of space and excellent taste in hiking trails."

Cerys laughed, but it came out broken, more breath than sound. "And if you ever decide you want to crew on a catamaran... this captain would be honored."

His lips quirked in a sad smile. "Yeah?"

"Yeah."

They both knew neither offer would be accepted. Not now.

Liam pulled her close, and Cerys let herself sink into him one last time—memorizing the solid warmth of his chest, the steady rhythm of his heartbeat against her cheek, the way his arms made the world feel both smaller and safer. The salt-and-sun smell of him. The weight of his chin resting on top of her head.

"For what it's worth," he murmured against her hair, his voice dropping to barely above a whisper, "*ataahua*, you're going to be extraordinary out there."

She held on tighter, her fingers curling into his shirt, knowing that when she let go, this would be over. That the moment she loosened her grip, he would climb back into his dinghy and motor away, and she would watch his silhouette disappear into the twilight.

Knowing she had to let go anyway.

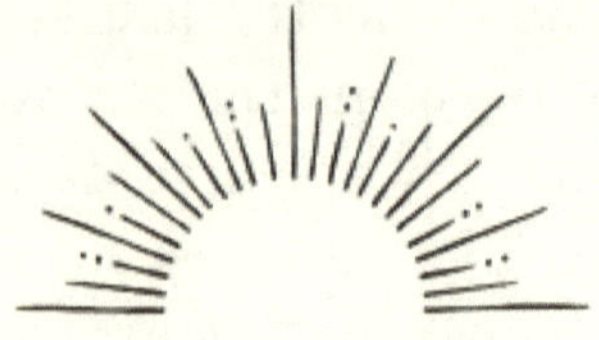

Chapter 15

The catamaran swayed gently at anchor, the morning sun already warm on the fiberglass deck. Cerys moved through her pre-departure checklist with the kind of focus that came from needing something—anything—to occupy her hands. Tighten the rigging turnbuckles. Check the halyard tension. Coil the dock lines she wouldn't need until the next port.

Her fingers worked automatically, muscle memory from months of solo sailing taking over while her mind circled the same worn groove: the way Liam had looked at her in the cockpit four nights ago. The weight of his arms around her. The empty space he'd left behind.

She crouched at the starboard bow, testing the shackle pin with her thumb. Solid. The boat was ready.

She wasn't.

What if this is the biggest mistake of your life?

The question surfaced again. She straightened, breath tight, and wiped her palms on her shorts. One task at a time. Check the windlass. Top off water. Stow the fenders.

By mid-morning, she'd exhausted every excuse. The dinghy's outboard buzzed as she motored toward Arohanui.

The town dock was already alive—fishermen offloading morning catch, kids cannonballing off the pier, a crackling Taviani pop song drifting from someone's radio. She tied off and shouldered her canvas bags. The familiar rhythm of the place settled over her. This island had given her so much: confidence, clarity, a version of herself she'd forgotten existed.

And Liam.

Near the fuel pumps, Paiwai stood deep in conversation with *Matāni* Atamai. The elder gestured as he spoke, posture relaxed but commanding—the kind of presence that made even casual conversations feel weighted.

Cerys slowed, not wanting to intrude. But *Matāni* Atamai's gaze found hers before she could slip past, his lined face breaking into a warm smile.

"*Ata mārie, e Cerys, kei te whakarite koe mō tō wehenga atu?*"

She glanced at Paiwai, who was already grinning. "Good morning, Cerys. You prepared for your leaving?"

"*Ae.*" She lifted the canvas bags slightly, their weight biting into her palms. Produce and provisions, dried goods, and fuel canisters. Everything she'd need for the next leg.

Matāni Atamai spoke again, his voice carrying that steady weight that made even practical advice feel like prophecy. "*Kua kī atu au ki te whānau Karaka kia nui ngā huawhenua pai mōu. Kāore e nui ngā huawhenua kei te wāhi e haere ana koe."*

Paiwai hopped down into her dinghy with practiced ease, the small boat rocking under his weight. "He told the Karaka family to load you up with vegetables. Says there won't be many where you're headed."

"Tell him thank you." Cerys shifted the canvas bags against her hip. "I'm well-stocked. Hopefully the weather holds."

Paiwai and *Matāni* Atamai spoke rapidly in Taviani, the syllables flowing too fast for her to catch. Something in the elder's tone made her stomach tighten.

Paiwai's grin faded. "Reach your destination before the third night. Then hunker down. Big storm coming."

Matāni Atamai stepped closer. His weathered hand cupped her cheek—the gesture of a grandfather, warm and grounding. He spoke again, softer this time, words she couldn't understand but felt anyway.

He dropped his hand and walked back down the dock, footsteps steady against the weathered planks.

"*Haere rā, Matāni* Atamai," she called after him.

When she turned back, Paiwai was grinning again—that knowing expression that made her both suspicious and hopeful. "Good news. He says the weather will be perfect when you and Liam return next year." A pause. "Also—take care of our Liam."

The words hit harder than they should. "But Liam's going back to America. And I'm not."

Paiwai's smile deepened. "*Matāni* Atamai always knows."

• • •

In the pre-dawn darkness of the next day, Liam stood in the center of his beach house, surrounded by half-packed bags that seemed to belong to someone else's life. The faint glow of approaching sunrise barely touched the horizon. Each object felt like a small betrayal. Evidence of the choice he was making.

Of the woman he was walking away from.

He picked up the mug, turned it over in his hands. Set it down. Picked it up again.

The creak of the front porch boards made him turn. Paiwai stood in the doorway, backlit by the dim glow of the porch light, his lined face barely visible in the shadows.

"Liam." His uncle's voice was quiet, but it carried. "Still as set in your ways as the day you first came home."

Liam gestured toward the couch—an invitation—then moved to the windows overlooking the dark ocean. "My parents are aging. The business needs—"

"My brother wasn't the first of our family to leave. Our great-great-uncle left this island to seek adventure," Paiwai said, moving into the room with that unhurried grace that made every step feel purposeful. "So our people could flourish beyond these shores. Kae studies medicine in New Zealand for the same reason." He paused, letting the words settle. "Exploration is in our blood, Liam. But so is returning home."

Liam turned from the window, meeting the elder's steady gaze.

"You are meant to explore," Paiwai continued. "To find passion. To let yourself want something beyond duty." His eyes held Liam's. "And to return home. With Cerys."

Her name hit like a physical blow.

Liam's hands tightened on the windowsill. The image arrived without permission: Cerys at the helm, hair wild in the wind, that fierce joy lighting her face as she sailed away. Away from him. From them.

Could he really just let her go?

The question crashed over him—the one he'd been dodging for days. What if he didn't have to choose? What if there was a third option, one he'd been too rigid to see?

Certainty snapped into focus.

"Uncle," his voice came out rough. "*Māuruuru koe mo tōu ārahitanga.*"

He was moving before he finished speaking, grabbing his keys from the counter, his feet already carrying him toward the door.

"If you'll excuse me—I have a boat to catch."

He was out the door and down the beach path before his uncle could respond, his bare feet pounding against weathered planks, splinters biting into his soles. Salt air burned his lungs. The taste of brine sharp on his tongue. No plan. No carefully prepared explanation for his parents. No contingency for what came after.

Just the bone-deep certainty that his uncle was right.

Cerys was his future. And he was about to let her disappear over the horizon.

He spotted her catamaran in the pre-dawn gray, her silhouette on the bow. Even from here, he could see the set of her shoulders—determined, heartbroken, brave.

"Cerys!" His voice carried across the still water, rough with urgency. "Wait!"

"Liam?" She dropped the anchor remote, the clatter sharp against the quiet morning water, and scrambled down the side decks to the back transom. Her heart hammered. "What are you doing here?"

He cut his engine. The sudden silence felt too loud.

He threw a line, tied off, and jumped aboard—all muscle memory, no hesitation. Then his hands were on her face and he was kissing her like he'd been holding his breath for days.

When he pulled back, his forehead pressed to hers, his words came low and rough. "I need six months." He swallowed hard. "Six months to close things out in America. And then—" His voice dropped lower. "Then I'm yours. If you still want me."

Her breath caught. Surprise flickered across her face, then confusion. Then something fragile and bright—hope.

She opened her mouth. Closed it. Her eyes searched his face like she was looking for the catch.

"What?" Her voice broke. "Really?"

He nodded, holding her gaze. His thumb traced her jawline, grounding himself in the moment. Six months felt like an eternity. What if she changed? What if the horizon pulled her so far away she forgot what this felt like?

But he'd already made his choice. Whatever came next, they'd face it together.

She let out a shaky laugh, tears slipping free. Then slowly—so slowly it nearly killed him—she nodded back.

He pulled her close, and this time when their lips met, it wasn't goodbye. It was a promise. An anchor. The beginning of something they'd both been too afraid to name.

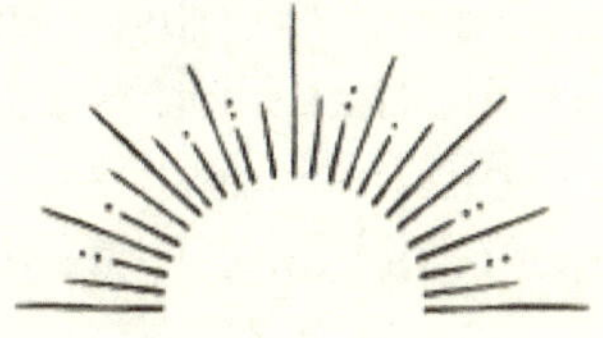

Chapter 16

Six months later (give or take a day...)

Cerys sailed toward Mo'orea with the wind steady at her back and the horizon clean ahead. Open water, open sky—just the way she liked it. Her catamaran cut through the swells with easy precision, responding to every touch of the wheel like an extension of her own body.

But as the island's green peaks sharpened against the blue, anticipation tightened in her chest. Another anchorage, yes. Another adventure, absolutely. But this time, something—someone—was waiting.

Six months. Six months of crackling phone calls, where half the words got lost in static. Pixelated video chats where his face froze mid-smile. Carefully worded emails that never quite captured what she meant to say. Each one had been a lifeline, proof that what they'd built on Mairana Nui could survive distance and time zones and all the ordinary life that filled the space between.

But what if it couldn't survive *this*—the actual reunion, the weight of expectation, the harsh light of reality?

What if the island glow had faded for him? What if their romance, so vivid in salt air and starlight, felt different now that he'd spent months back in the real world?

The worry was irrational. She knew that. Liam had given her no reason to doubt. Every call, every message, every "I'm counting down the days" had been steady. Sure.

But fear didn't care about logic.

She adjusted the helm, gaze settling on the water. Sunlight shattered across the surface in a thousand shifting fragments. Salt air filled her lungs. The rhythm of the waves steadied her breathing—rise, fall, rise.

They'd made promises. She had to trust them.

Mo'orea drew closer, lush peaks softening in the afternoon haze. Hands sure on the wheel, she guided her catamaran toward the channel and felt resolve settle into her bones.

Whatever came next, she'd face it. With courage. With an open heart.

No longer just the solo sailor, chasing horizons alone.

Someone who'd chosen to let another person in. And that terrified her almost as much as it thrilled her.

Sails retracted, motor fired up, she navigated the narrow strait into a stunning turquoise lagoon. The water shifted from deep cobalt to pale aquamarine as she entered the protected bay, mountains rising green and dramatic beyond. Anchor down. Engine off. The sudden quiet settled around her like a held breath, broken only by water slapping against the hulls and the distant cry of seabirds.

Post-sail checklist: inspect the anchor set, rinse salt from her skin, tidy the salon. The tasks moved through her on autopilot, her mind already elsewhere, her hands finding their rhythm in familiar work.

By early afternoon, she'd powered up her laptop and made herself tea. Winter had arrived in the South Pacific—the day carried an unexpected chill that crept through the cabin despite the sun overhead. A light sweater pulled on, she wrapped her hands around the warm mug.

Footage began downloading from her SD cards, the files populating slowly across her screen. The progress bar crawled forward while she waited, listening to rigging creak overhead.

Inserting a new card into her camera, she turned it on and pushed record. "Hello everyone! I just made it to my anchorage in Maharepa." She gestured toward the view beyond the salon windows—green peaks, turquoise water, a scattering of other boats at anchor. "Spent some time getting settled because it's time to come clean."

The sound of a boat approaching caused her to stop. She moved out of the saloon and walked to the bow, camera still rolling. "I've been keeping a bit of a secret from everyone. And in just a moment you're all going to know what it is."

She flipped the camera around and focused it on a small boat heading her way. On board was a familiar figure and another man operating the boat. Her heart kicked hard against her ribs. "New Horizons is getting a new permanent crew member. And is that..." She zoomed in on the boat, laughter bubbling up. "It is! He brought a case of hot sauce. O-M-jeez, I love this man."

As the boat came closer, Cerys couldn't help but wave enthusiastically, the camera shaking in her excitement. The sight of Liam—standing there with that broad grin, windblown and real and *here*, holding a box of her favorite hot sauce like a trophy—was more than she could have wished for. "We're going to new horizons, everyone," she said, her voice breaking slightly. "And new adventures."

She stopped the recording and moved to the stern transom, her hands trembling as she set the camera down. The smaller boat drew alongside, rocking gently in the swell, and Liam didn't wait for it to fully stop—he leaped aboard with practiced ease, finding his balance instantly on the shifting deck.

"*Mālō e lelei, ataahua,*" he said, arms already reaching for her. His voice was rough, warm, everything she'd been missing. "I've missed you."

Cerys rushed into his embrace, laughing as the impact nearly knocked them both off balance. The boat rocked beneath them, finding new equilibrium. For a moment, she just held him—solid and real and *here*, smelling of salt and sun and something distinctly him. "*Ipo,*" she whispered against his chest, feeling his heart beat steady and strong. "I can't believe you're actually here."

He pulled back just enough to look at her, his thumb brushing her cheek with deliberate tenderness. "Believe it."

They worked quickly to transfer his belongings—duffel bags, equipment cases, and yes, an entire box of her favorite hot sauce. The boat operator helped pass items across, steady and efficient. As he waved goodbye and motored away, his wake sent gentle ripples across the turquoise water.

The sudden quiet settled around them again, but this time it felt different. Fuller. The hulls creaked softly. Rigging clinked overhead. Water lapped at the transoms in an easy rhythm.

Cerys looked up from the deck at Liam standing there—six months of aching distance collapsing into this single, sun-drenched moment. Afternoon light caught in his dark eyes; salt had dried in his hair like a crown. That look—the one that had haunted her every night—was back, intense and unguarded.

"Are you hungry?" she asked, pulse already racing.

"Starving." Voice rough, like he'd been holding the word in his throat for months.

He closed the distance deliberately. Hand cupped her face; thumb brushed her cheekbone. She leaned into it, eyes fluttering closed.

"Thought about this every damn day," he murmured.

"Me too."

The first kiss was soft—tentative, relearning curves and taste. Then it deepened, hungry. Arms around his neck, she pressed closer. His hands settled at her waist, thumbs stroking bare skin under her dress hem.

They broke apart, breathing hard. Foreheads together.

"Inside?" she whispered.

He nodded.

She led him down into the cabin. The space felt smaller, warmer—sun-baked air thick already. When she turned, his gaze tracked her with that steady focus that always made her feel stripped bare in the best way.

His fingers found her dress hem, grazing thighs. She didn't stop him. He lifted her easily; she laughed in surprise, the sound melting into a sigh as he laid her on the bed and settled between her thighs. The catamaran swayed gently, rigging creaking overhead like a heartbeat.

"Your smile," he said quietly, forehead to hers. "Kept me going. You have no idea how much I need this. Need you."

She widened her legs, rolled her hips against the growing hardness. Cabin air turned heavy, sun-warmed. "Show me then. Nice and slow."

He kissed her deeply—tongue deliberate, claiming. When he pulled back, they were gasping. She pulled him down again, tracing his lips before pushing inside. He groaned, taking control, the kiss turning almost punishing.

He rolled them so she straddled him. Mattress shifted with the boat's gentle rock. Hands roamed—one sliding under her dress to pull underwear aside, cupping her ass to grind her against him; the other reaching up to unclasp her bra, freeing her breasts.

She sat up, hands on his waistband. He lifted hips; she tugged pants down. They both groaned as she wrapped fingers around him—hot, thick, real after so many months of fantasy.

"Finally," she whispered, voice catching. "I've missed you so much."

His mouth curved—slow, wicked. "Then show me, *ataahua*. Ride me nice and slow. Let me feel how much you've missed having me inside you."

The words sent heat flaring. She reached for the drawer, found the condom. His hands steadied her hips as she rolled it on, then positioned herself.

When she began to sink down—slow, savoring the stretch, the fullness—his fingers tightened, eyes locked on hers.

"*Aroha au iā koe,*" he rasped, voice thick with emotion and want. The words in his native tongue hit her like a wave—he'd chosen them deliberately, carrying the weight of everything he was.

She met his gaze, breath hitching. "I love you," she whispered back, barely audible over the lap of water and creak of rigging.

She took her time lowering fully, hips rolling in small circles once seated. The boat swayed; they matched its rhythm—rise and fall, slow and deep. His hands guided her—one on her hip, the other sliding up her spine.

"So fucking perfect," he murmured. "Feel how deep you take me? How wet you are for me after all this time? Been dreaming about this tight heat gripping my cock."

She braced on his chest, feeling his heartbeat thunder beneath her palm. Sweat gathered where skin met skin—salt, ocean, them. Eyes locked, everything else faded: distant gulls, neighboring boats, the world. Only this—bodies moving together, breath mingling, the steady creak of her home holding them.

He thrust up to meet her on each downstroke—controlled, devastating. One hand slipped between them, fingers circling her clit with maddening precision.

"That's it," he growled. "Let me feel you fall apart. Then I'll fill you up just like I've wanted to for months."

The orgasm built slow, then crashed—deep waves rolling through her core, chest, throat. She clenched around him; he followed with a guttural sound, hips snapping up as he shuddered through it.

They collapsed tangled together, skin cooling in the sun-trapped warmth. Afternoon light shifted through the porthole, golden on water.

His fingers traced lazy patterns on her back. She nestled against his chest, listening to his heartbeat slow.

She propped up to look at him. “Amazing start on making up for lost time,” she said, breathless, smiling. “Any regrets?”

He shook his head, pulling her closer. “Not one, *ataahua*. This... it feels exactly right.“ Voice warm, content. “Wouldn’t change a thing.”

The words settled deep. Six months of doubt dissolved here, in a Mo’orea lagoon, his arms around her.

“Good,” she whispered. Lips brushed his—soft, lingering. “Welcome home.”

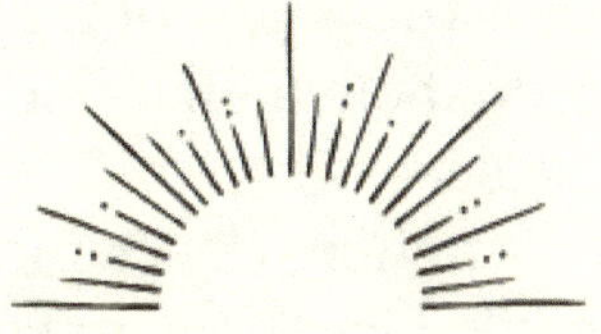

Epilogue

Several months had passed since Liam joined her aboard New Horizons. They'd settled into a rhythm—anticipating each other's movements, trusting calls without hesitation, working as one unit.

Today, they were navigating toward Urquharts Bay, near New Zealand—a tricky approach with high winds and shallow patches near the entrance. Wind howled through the rigging. The bow slapped against short, angry chop, each impact jolting through the hulls.

Liam stood at the helm, eyes scanning the path ahead. Cerys positioned herself at the bow as lookout, one hand braced against the rail, salt spray stinging her cheeks.

"Starboard, ten degrees!" she called.

His hands moved smoothly on the wheel.

Inside the bay's calmer waters, the wind dropped. Green hills rose steeply on either side, dotted with native bush that glowed in the afternoon light. A handful of other boats swung on their anchors, scattered across the protected basin like seeds.

They dropped anchor. Cerys moved through the post-sail checks while Liam dove to confirm the anchor was set. The familiar routine grounded them.

After showers that washed away salt and exhaustion, they gravitated to the salon. Liam worked at the galley preparing lunch, the fresh mahi mahi they'd caught earlier sizzling on the induction grill. Cerys settled at her laptop to download footage from their SD cards.

The scent of cooking fish mingled with sea air. Through the open hatch came the cry of gulls and the creak of rigging. She glanced up from her screen.

Six months ago, she would have done all of this alone. The thought wasn't bitter—just observational. She'd built a life around solo self-sufficiency, proving she could handle everything alone. And she had. But having someone to share the helm with, to call out bearings to, to cook lunch with after a challenging approach—choosing to sail with a partner felt like embracing abundance rather than accepting less.

"Hey, babe," she said. "What time are we meeting Kae and the others tomorrow?"

Liam looked up from the grill, considering. "After we document those ruins. I think our viewers are going to love it." He paused, his expression thoughtful. "So sometime in the afternoon."

Cerys nodded, her fingers resuming their dance across the keyboard. "It's awesome that Tama's band made it to the competition."

A low chuckle rumbled from Liam's chest as he flipped the fish. "Yeah. I'm excited to see Kae again. Hear about his studies." He turned slightly, catching her eye. "Are you sure about having Kae and Nahi sail back with us to Mairana Nui?"

She swiveled in her chair to face him fully, a soft smile on her lips. "Of course. They promised to help with boat repairs while we're there for cyclone season." She tilted her head. "Besides, it'll be nice to have company."

Through the open hatch, she could hear the distant cry of gulls and the metallic clink of someone working on their rigging two boats over. A light breeze carried the scent of native bush from the surrounding hills, earthy and green beneath the ever-present salt.

"Also," Liam grumbled, fetching fresh vegetables from the hanging basket, "it's a good excuse to not have that Myles kid tagging along."

His hands moved deftly, slicing tomatoes on the wooden cutting board. The rhythmic *thunk-thunk-thunk* of the knife filled the comfortable quiet between them.

"Add tomatoes and onions to the list," he said. "I'm using the last ones for today's salad."

"Got it." She turned back to her laptop, fingers hovering over the keys. A moment passed before she looked up at him again, her head tilting slightly. "And don't think I didn't catch on to what you were doing when you suggested it to Kae."

Her long twists tumbled over her shoulder as she fixed him with a knowing look. "You better be nice to him and Fin. The cave incident was a year ago. I thought Moanuins were all about forgiveness."

He shrugged, chopping steadily. “Don’t know who told you that.” A slight smirk tugged at his lips. “Besides, I’m only half Moanuin.”

Cerys laughed. She shook her head, twists shifting across her shoulders. “You’re impossible.” Her voice softened. “But I love you anyway.”

Back to her laptop. Through the open hatch, rigging clinked softly from a neighboring boat.

“That’s good to know,” Liam said, glancing over his shoulder. That barely-there smile appeared at the edges of his mouth. “Because I love you too. More than I ever thought possible.”

Their eyes held. Warmth spread through her chest—solid, unshakeable.

Liam’s phone buzzed on the counter. He glanced at the screen, then at Cerys. “It’s Paiti.” He tapped the speaker button.

“*Kia ora*, cousin!“ Paiti’s voice burst through the speakers. So loud they could probably hear her on land. “You two make it to Urquharts okay?”

“Yeah, we’re anchored,” Liam said, his tone amused. “What’s up?”

“So, quick update from paradise—your dad’s decided he’s moving in with my parents while you’re back on Mairana Nui. Says he doesn’t want to ‘intrude on the two lovebirds.’” She drew out the last words mockingly. “Which is sweet and all, but now I’ve got to deal with not only *my* dad, but *your* dad, *and* my mom—who is *your* aunt—dealing with her older brother being back home after however many years.”

Cerys bit back a laugh, watching Liam’s expression shift between fondness and exasperation.

"You know what that means, cuz?" Paiti continued without pause. "You owe me. Big time. I'm thinking you handle all the fish cleaning when you get here. For like, a month. No, two months."

"Paiti—" Liam started.

"Non-negotiable! I'm providing elder care for *your* family drama. Payment is due upon arrival." The line went dead.

Liam stared at his phone, then looked at Cerys. "She hung up on me."

"She did," Cerys confirmed, grinning.

Her own phone buzzed. She glanced down at the text notification and her smile faded slightly.

> *Hope you arrived safely, sweetheart. But honestly, do you really think you can raise a family on a boat? Call me when you get a chance.*
> *Love, Mom*

Cerys groaned. "I'm not even pregnant."

Liam looked up from the grill, that barely-there smile playing at his lips. "Yet."

She threw a dish towel at him. He caught it one-handed, chuckling.

The breeze shifted outside, carrying bush scent through the hatch. Whatever came next, they'd face it together.

A Note from Jade Black

Thank you so much for diving into the world of *Saltwater Between Us*. This story means the world to me as my debut, and I'm so glad you were part of the journey.

Craving more swoons, secrets, and happily-ever-afters?

Sign up to receive The Conservatory Letters for sneak peeks, romantic chaos, character confessions, trope deep dives, and early cover reveals.

Scan here or visit: https://bit.ly/inkbound-conservatory

About the author

Jade Black writes stories where love is powerful, complicated, and never an afterthought. Her work spans contemporary romance, epic gothic fantasy romance, and romantic suspense, blending emotional intensity with lush worldbuilding and high-stakes devotion.

Drawn to relationships forged in fire rather than convenience, Jade's stories explore identity, resilience, and the transformative nature of partnership. Her characters fall in love amid political intrigue, generational secrets, dangerous loyalties, and the quiet, everyday courage it takes to be fully seen. Romance, in her world, is not a subplot. It is the catalyst.

Influenced by gothic atmospheres, layered mythology, and the fragile line between vulnerability and strength, Jade crafts sweeping narratives where passion and power exist side by side. Whether set in a contemporary city or a crumbling empire, her stories promise emotional depth, immersive settings, and love stories that feel earned.

When not writing, Jade finds inspiration in art museums, architectural history, and the subtle choreography of human connection.

COMING SEPTEMBER 2026

Everything After

By Jade Black

One weekend in the city. One beautiful mistake. One secret that could shatter two careers.

Leiliana moved to the vibrant city of Fujiyako for a fresh start and a dream career at Spherestone. She's built a careful, quiet life—one she's determined to protect at any cost. But her world begins to unravel the moment she comes face-to-face with Kanakami Mishada.

He's the ruthless head of Sales, a corporate heir, and the man from a passionate Halloween weekend Leiliana has spent months trying to forget.

Now, trapped in the same glass towers and navigating high-stakes corporate sabotage, the unresolved chemistry between them is as chilling as a Fujiyako typhoon. Kanakami is looking for answers Leiliana isn't ready to give. Between glittering winter balls and cooling pumpkin spice lattes, they must decide if they are enemies by design... or if their "mistake" was the only real thing they've ever had.

Sneak Peek: Everything After

SEPTEMBER

Leiliana's fingers ached from gripping her purse strap. The September morning had barely begun, but Fujiyako was already alive—car horns layering over each other, buses rumbling past, voices scattering into the humid air. A transit announcement crackled overhead in Jiyokonian, the syllables blurring together too fast for her to catch more than a few words.

The train station thrummed with motion. Commuters in crisp business attire cut past her with the kind of speed that came from muscle memory, drawn toward the waiting train like it might leave without them. Leiliana stepped off the platform and into the current of it all, her phone already in her hand. The screen was blank. No new messages. She exhaled and slipped it back into her purse, the leather strap rough under her fingertips, then checked again thirty seconds later.

Steel and oil hung in the air, cut through with something sweeter—pastries from a kiosk she couldn't see. Her stomach twisted. She hadn't had time to get more than a couple hurried sips of her coffee down, and the bitterness still clung to the back of her throat. When had she last slept more than four hours straight? She couldn't remember. Leiliana closed her eyes for half a breath, swaying slightly as the crowd pressed around her—sleeves brushing her arms, the fabric of a dozen coats and shirts creating a shifting wall of texture—then forced them open and checked her phone again. The line at the kiosk had doubled. A sigh escaped her lips as the crowd pulled her forward instead, her heels clicking against worn stone, blending into the hum of a hundred other footsteps and the low whir of a train pulling away behind her.

The days were cooling off as autumn approached, yet the beginning rainy season blanketed Fujiyako in a thick humidity that wreaked havoc on Leiliana's naturally curly hair. An errant curl fell across her face. She tucked it behind her ear and sidestepped a slow-moving older couple, then paused, glancing back at them with a smile. The woman wore a fuchsia patterned blouse, her silver hair neatly pinned, while the man had weather-worn features and a warm, gravelly voice as he pointed out a passing car to his wife. Their warm smiles to one another stirred something sharp in her chest. Leiliana looked away, her throat tightening as she swallowed against the lump forming there. When she glanced back, the couple was still smiling at each other, and the ache spread wider.

Drawing a deep breath to calm the flutter of nerves about her first day at Spherestone, she nodded politely and called out, "How are you both today?"

Since moving to Jiyokon, she'd discovered that people warmed to her more quickly when she initiated conversation. She could almost hear her paternal grandmother's southern twang: "Good manners open doors that the finest education cannot."

The older woman's face brightened. "Oh, we're doing just fine! Made it all the way here to see our son. His wife's about to have our first grandbaby—any day now."

Something in Leiliana went still. *Grandbaby.* Her hand tightened on her purse strap, and for half a second, the photo she'd pulled up three times before the train had even left the station that moment flashed in her mind. Her throat tightened. *Not now. Not here.* But the ache was already spreading, that familiar mix of longing and guilt that made her want to check again, to see that little face one more time, to make sure everything was okay even though she'd only left an hour ago. She forced herself to breathe. To smile. To stay present. The older woman was still beaming at her, waiting for a response, and Leiliana blinked hard, pulling herself back to the moment before the feeling could crack her wide open.

"That's—wow, uh, how wonderful."

They came to a stop at a street corner, waiting for the light to change. Fujiyako sprawled around them in perpetual motion—businesspeople with practiced indifference, schoolchildren in crisp uniforms, tourists caught between wonder and overwhelm.

"Yes, yes," the older man nodded, chest swelling with pride. "First time in the city for my wife. We came to help out and celebrate." He turned his kind eyes to Leiliana. "How about you, young lady? You're not from around here either, are you?"

"I'm doing—yeah, I'm great, actually. On my way to start my new job at Spherestone. First day." She adjusted her purse strap, felt the words tumbling out a little too fast. "I moved here last month from Kimobiro prefecture, so I'm still—anyway, congratulations. That's really wonderful. So happy for your family."

She waved as she turned away, a slight bounce in her step despite the flutter of nerves in her stomach—and the tightness that hadn't quite left her chest. As she walked the final blocks toward Spherestone, she mentally rehearsed her introduction to her new team, but her thoughts kept snagging. Would they find her qualifications impressive enough? She'd worked so hard for this opportunity—her first position at a prestigious tech company after years of grinding through her education and freelance work. This was her chance to establish a steady income, the kind of security she desperately needed.

Especially now that someone very important was depending on her.

She rounded the last corner and stopped.

The Tateshina building cut into the sky—forty floors of glass and steel that threw the morning sun back at her like a challenge. Spherestone occupied the top dozen floors. She'd memorized that detail weeks ago, along with the floor plan, the department heads' names, the train routes. Anything to feel prepared.

Her phone buzzed in her purse. She pulled it out—just a spam notification—and her thumb hovered over her messages before she shoved it back down. The cheap plastic case felt slick against her palm. Not now.

Across the street, a coffee shop hummed with the pre-work rush. The smell hit her first—dark roast, butter, something cinnamon-sweet that made her stomach clench. She checked her watch. Still early. She could stop. Just for a minute.

The display case gleamed behind the window: croissants splitting open with steam, muffins fat with berries, cookies stacked like promises. Her hand drifted toward her purse before the numbers surfaced in her mind. Rent. Daycare deposit. Formula. The move had gutted her savings, and every yen between now and her first paycheck was already spoken for. Fingertips pressed against the cool glass for just a second. Then pulled away.

"Soon," she whispered, forcing herself to step back. First paycheck. She'd come back then. Maybe make it a Friday thing—surviving the week earned you something sweet. A delivery truck rumbled past, its side panel covered in bold Jiyokonian characters advertising something she couldn't quite make out.

The Tateshina building pulled her focus back. Shoulders straightened. One foot, then the other. The pavement was uneven in places where the city had patched it over. A salaryman brushed past, his suit jacket grazing her arm, and she caught a whiff of cigarette smoke mixed with cologne.

New chapter. Best foot forward.

Her heart was beating too fast. She'd barely slept.

And someone very small was counting on her not to mess this up.

• • •

There's More Where This Came From.

Saltwater Between Us is just one corner of the world I'm building.

I write across genres under different names – because some stories need salt air and heartbreak, and others need something stranger and darker.

If you want to know what's coming next (and get the occasional behind-the-scenes confession from a writer running on caffeine and chaos):

Join The Inkbound Circle.

Monthly dispatches. Works-in-progress. Bonus stories. No spam. No nonsense. Just magic.

www.inkboundrealms.com/newsletter-sign-up

– Jade Black

www.ingramcontent.com/pod-product-compliance
Lightning Source LLC
LaVergne TN
LVHW050956080826
845145LV00009B/2322

* 9 7 8 1 9 7 1 2 2 7 0 3 0 *